A.J.'S ANGEL

WILDE'S BOOK 3

L.A. WITT

Copyright Information

A.J.'s Angel

Second edition

Copyright © 2010, 2017, 2020 L.A. Witt

First edition published by Samhain Publishing, 2010-2017.

Cover Art by Lori Witt

Editor: Linda Ingmanson

ISBN: 978-1543056921

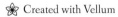 Created with Vellum

To everyone who ever said I couldn't.

ABOUT A.J.'S ANGEL

Luke Emerson is the last person Sebastian Wakefield
expects to see strolling into his tattoo shop. But Luke's not
back after four years to take up where they left off. Not even
to apologize for the cheating that broke them up.

Luke wants a custom tattoo, a memorial for someone known
only as "A.J." Much as Seb would love to tell Luke to take
this ink and shove it, he's a professional. Plus, he's reluctant
to admit, he wouldn't mind getting his hands on Luke again.
Even if it's just business.

Once Luke's in the tattoo chair, though, Seb finds himself
struggling with all the anger and resentment he thought
he'd left behind—and those aren't the only feelings
reignited. Their relationship may have been turbulent, but
it was also passionate. Four years clearly hasn't been long
enough for the embers of that fire to go cold.

A few subtle hints from Luke is all it takes to make Seb

consider indulging in some of that physical passion. It shouldn't be that tough to keep his emotions from getting tangled up in sweaty sheets.

After all, it's not like he's in love with Luke anymore. Right?

This 35,000 word novella was previously published.

CHAPTER 1

THERE WERE DOZENS OF TATTOO SHOPS WITHIN A hundred mile radius of Seattle, and Luke Emerson chose to come waltzing through the front door of mine.

It was a damned good thing I wasn't with a client right then. It was midday, midweek, so we weren't all that busy, and when the bell above the door jingled over Jason's buzzing tattoo needle, I had my feet on a desk and my nose in a trade magazine.

Fortunately, that meant I didn't screw up a tattoo or injure someone when I nearly jumped out of my skin. Unfortunately, it also meant I was conspicuously *not* busy. Slimeball ex-boyfriend or not, he had to be treated like a potential client, particularly since there was another client present.

I set my magazine down and dropped my feet to the floor. On the way across the short expanse of space between us, I supposed I could have looked anywhere but right at him until I absolutely had to. But no, I used that time, those few steps, to force myself to get used to the sight of him. To drink in what I'd hoped never to see again.

Damn it, why did he still have to be so good-looking even after all these years? Time and again I'd wished on him a beer gut, a rapidly receding hairline, or at least a generous helping of gray hair. Preferably all three. Sure, it was petty and childish, but giving myself a laugh over it beat the hell out of hurting.

My wish wasn't granted. Four years had chiseled away some of the youthful roundness of his features, leaving him with cheekbones nearly as sharp as his jaw. His dark hair was still thick and full without a strand of gray in sight. His sleeves, rolled to just below his elbows, revealed sculpted, lightly bronzed forearms. It would be just my luck that every last inch of him was equally toned and tanned.

Then there were his eyes. Those damned beautiful ice blue eyes. They hadn't lost a bit of the intensity that had always made me weak in the knees, but I refused to allow them to have that effect on me now.

I wasn't the only one doing a little drinking in. He made no effort to hide the slow down-up of his eyes, nor was he subtle about the pauses. Once at the tattoos making up my mostly finished right sleeve. Then at the long-since-completed left sleeve. My face. An upward flick to my eyes then a little higher. Wry amusement curled his lips, probably at the sight of my eyebrow ring. He'd always loved my penchant for ink and piercings. Too much of a self-described wimp to get any of his own, but he'd certainly been enamored of mine.

As he looked me over again, I wondered if he was trying to imagine what new ink work and jewelry I hid beneath my clothes. Several more tattoos and a pair of gold hoops, but he didn't need to know that.

Our eyes met again, and an instant later, he dropped his

gaze. Not out of shyness, though. Not even close, considering that dropped gaze went straight below my belt.

Subtle, Luke. Real subtle.

I cleared my throat and casually jammed a hand into the pocket of my jeans. "Long time no see."

He looked up, not even a flicker of embarrassment in his expression. "Yeah, it's been a while, hasn't it?"

Not nearly long enough, I decided, but I forced myself to stay cordial. "So, what brings you into my shop?"

He grinned, making sure to flash his straight, gleaming teeth, every last one of which I wanted to knock out of his head. "I'm interested in getting a tattoo."

Oh? "Open for Business" above your ass? Or "Village Bicycle" on your dick?

"Well, you've come to the right place." I shifted my weight. "What did you have in mind?"

He took a breath, and I swear he set those broad shoulders back a little more. A gesture of arrogance? Nerves? I couldn't be sure.

"I want..." He paused, dropping his gaze for a split second. "Um, it'll be a custom design."

"Oh." I saw my escape, even if it was a lie, and jumped on it. "Well, that's more Jason's territory than mine, so—"

"No."

I blinked.

Luke shook his head. "I want you to design it. And put it on."

I glanced at Jason and his client then lowered my voice and eyed Luke. "Why me?"

"Because I like your work." He grinned again. "I always have, you know that."

"I'm also not the only artist in town." My eyes narrowed. "As you well know."

He flinched and looked at the counter between us. "Sebastian, please. This one is important to me. I wouldn't let anyone else do it."

I clenched my jaw. A million barbs rested on the tip of my tongue, ready to demand to know why he thought I should give a flying fuck how important this tattoo was to him, or how much he respected my work, or any of that. But professionalism prevailed, if only because my business partner and a paying client were within earshot. That, and business had been slow lately. Jason and I needed every penny we could bring into this place right now.

I sighed and reached under the counter to get a sketchbook. "Okay, what is it?"

He dug a piece of folded paper out of his back pocket. He didn't unfold it yet, but gestured with it as he said, "It'll be something like this, but with a name above it."

I managed to keep from flinching. *Finally decided to settle down with someone?* I thought bitterly. *Or is this the first name in a guestbook?* I barely kept myself from snickering at that thought in spite of the jealousy—no, *bitterness*. It was nothing but bitterness. It was anger that tightened my chest and turned my stomach. That, and maybe a little pity for whatever sorry bastard was being immortalized on Luke's person.

No jealousy whatsoever.

I held out my hand for the piece of paper.

"Anything else?" I asked through gritted teeth, unfolding the paper and bracing myself for the inevitable gloating about his new man, his soul mate, or his flavor of the month. I wondered how appreciative he'd be if I mentioned I'd never actually drawn a douche bag on someone's skin, but I'd be open to doing so if that—

My heart fell into my feet when I realized what the

design was. An intricately drawn, elaborately shaded and stunningly beautiful...angel. Looking heavenward. Clutching a folded American flag to her chest.

Oh, crap.

"It's, um..." He paused again. "A memorial tattoo."

Inwardly, I cringed, wishing the ground would swallow me up for even thinking what I had. I cleared my throat. "I'm, uh, I'm sorry to hear it." So many questions. So many things I probably didn't want to know. I tapped my pen on the sketchbook. "Where do you want it?"

He gestured at his left upper arm, and I fought to keep from shivering. At least it wasn't going on his shoulders. His arms were spectacular, but the man had the kind broad, powerful shoulders that *almost* made up for what a dick he was.

I muffled a cough. "Okay, so, this design..." I gestured at the piece of paper.

"Something close to it, anyway. Doesn't have to be exactly the same."

I raised an eyebrow. "Do you want it changed in any particular way?"

He looked at the picture for a moment. "No, not really. I mean, it's fine as is, but, you know, if you want to do anything with it, be my guest." He swallowed, and when he met my eyes again, any humor or taunting was gone. I wondered if it had been there at all, or if I'd superimposed them myself.

"And the name?" I asked.

"Just A.J. is fine," he said quietly.

"Any preference for the writing? Font, anything like that?"

"No, not really." He offered a smile that might have been genuine. "You're the artist."

"Do you want the years? Birth and..." I paused.

His eyebrows flicked upward. "Death?"

I nodded.

"I'm not sure yet," he said. "Is that something I can add later?"

"Yeah, of course." I made a few notes on my sketchpad. Then I gestured at the angel drawing. "Do you mind if I hang on to this, or do—"

"Go ahead. I have another copy."

I slipped the drawing into my sketchpad. "I guess that's all I need to know about the design, then." I fought to keep my annoyance out of my voice. He was here to put money in my pocket, he'd obviously lost someone dear to him, but that didn't change the fact that he'd put me through the wringer a few years ago. There was more to this. There had to be.

There had to be more, and as long as we were in my professional territory with colleague and client nearby, I couldn't ask.

"You're looking at about three hours." I took a breath. "So, three hundred dollars."

He didn't even blink. "I'll pay cash."

"Okay." I paused. "You can either do it all at once, or you can break it into two appointments." *All at once. All at once. For the love of God, all at once. Let's just get this thing over with.*

A grin, or possibly a nervous laugh, played at the corners of his mouth. "I guess I don't know how much of a wimp I'll be, so why don't we do two appointments?"

"Most people prefer to get it done in one shot," I said. "If it turns out to be more painful than they expected, they're often hesitant to come back for the second appointment." *Which would just break my heart. Really. It would.*

"I'll take my chances with two." He winked. The arrogant son of a bitch actually winked.

"Customer's always right," I said with a shrug.

He chuckled. "Let's book it, then."

Can't fucking wait. I reached under the counter again, this time for the tattered binder that passed for an appointment book.

"Let me see what I have available." I flipped to the correct page and ran my finger down the list of time slots. Some were filled, some weren't, and every gap in the schedule reminded me why I couldn't afford to turn his sorry ass away. The landlord didn't care if the rent money came from my ex-boyfriend or the Pope as long as he got paid.

Luke craned his neck to see the calendar. "What about Friday night? Looks like you have an opening around seven." Our eyes met. He smiled, and if I didn't know him as well as I did, I'd have thought it was an innocent, even demure expression. With a one-shouldered shrug, he added, "That'll give it time to heal over the weekend so it's not bugging me so much at work."

"It won't heal in two days," I said through my teeth.

"No, but most of the sting will be gone by then, won't it?" He paused. "You always said the first day or two were the worst."

"So I did," I muttered. "Seven o'clock on Friday, then?"

"That'll work."

I turned to Jason. "Hey, you mind closing for me on Saturday if I close on Friday?"

Jason glanced up from the nearly completed tiger on his client's leg. "Yeah, no problem. I was going to ask if you wanted to switch anyway."

"Oh, well, that's perfect, then," Luke said, and I didn't have to look to know he was grinning.

I released a long breath through my nose. "Thanks, man," I said flatly.

Jason cocked his head, an unspoken question furrowing his brow. Ever the professional, though, he didn't say a thing. He dipped his needle in some ink and went back to work.

I turned back to my ex. "Friday at seven it is." I wrote *L. Emerson* in the seven o'clock blank and drew an arrow through the next three thirty-minute time slots. "I also need your phone number. In case anything changes."

"Right, of course." He recited his number and I wrote it next to his name.

"What about the second appointment?" I asked.

"Hmm." He looked at my calendar again. "How long does it need to heal before you work on it again?"

"I'd give it about two weeks so the scab has time to completely fall off."

He grimaced. "Lovely."

"Par for the course."

"Then I guess two weeks from this one."

After Jason—the cooperative bastard—confirmed he didn't mind switching yet another Friday and Saturday, I wrote Luke in and closed the appointment book.

"Well," Luke said, flashing me that toothy grin once again, "I guess it's a date."

I offered a thin-lipped smile. "Something like that."

He took a step back from the counter, making a casual gesture toward the door. "I should let you get back to work. I'll see you on Friday night."

"Yeah. See you then."

He smiled, probably hoping I'd do the same. When I

didn't, he laughed quietly, narrowing his eyes as if I was the punch line of a joke no one heard but Luke-fucking-Emerson.

He turned to go. A second later, the bell above the door jingled, and I exhaled hard.

"You okay, Seb?" Jason asked.

I nodded. "Yeah, I'm fine." I shoved the appointment book under the counter and put my sketchbook under my arm.

"Did you know that guy or something?"

I blew out another breath. "You could say that, yeah." I looked over my shoulder. "You mind if I take a break?"

He reached for his workstation to put more ink on his needle. "No, no, go ahead."

I must have looked more rattled than I thought. Jason usually gave me hell about taking breaks on slow days. Of course they were state-mandated, but we were always ribbing each other about anything and everything, and taking a break when there was nothing to do anyway was a frequent target.

I went into the back office and closed the door, shutting out the white noise of Jason's tattoo needle. I dropped into the rickety, faux leather swivel chair behind the desk. Leaning back, I rubbed my eyes with my thumb and forefinger.

Four years. I hadn't seen his face in four goddamned years, and out of the blue, he marches into my shop like he has every right to be here.

And in two days, three hours and forty-one minutes, he'd be here again. A scheduled, paying customer who *did* have every right to be here.

I groaned and stared up at the ceiling. So many questions. So many things I needed to know and didn't want to know. So much I wanted to say once we were alone in two days, three hours and forty minutes.

Nerves coiled and tightened the pit of my stomach. I hadn't expected to see his face again this side of Armageddon, but what surprised me even more than his presence was the effect he'd had on me. Sure, I hadn't gone a day without thinking about him. The anger had lingered—if I let myself, I could still wallow in his memory and work myself up until I saw red—but time had tempered it. Dimmed the glowing embers without letting them die completely.

And with the jingle of the door's bells, every last one of those embers had flared to life, and I'd loathed him with all the fervor of the day he'd walked out of the apartment we'd shared. From the second he'd stepped out of my past and into my shop, I was off balance. I'd lost my footing, and I wondered when the hell I'd find it again.

I'd told myself I was over him. After all this time, I had to be. But seeing his face, seeing that smug grin when he knew I couldn't and wouldn't throw him out, made it clear I was only kidding myself.

Over him or not, I was now committed—twice—to an hour and a half of being in his presence. An hour and a half in close proximity. Ninety fucking minutes with my hands on his skin, even if there would be a thin layer of latex to shield me from making actual, unnervingly intimate contact. Nowhere to run, nowhere to hide, and nothing to do but tattoo A.J.'s angel on his arm.

At least I wasn't still attracted to him. No way, no how. I had no desire to see if he was still as toned and tanned as he'd been back then. I hadn't given a moment's thought to whether or not he still wore that spicy cologne, or if he'd still get goose bumps if my lower lip brushed just beneath his ear. I certainly wasn't the least bit curious if he still kissed like that.

I was *not* still attracted to him.

I sighed. Something told me I wouldn't be getting a lot of sleep between now and seven o'clock on Friday night.

Two days.

Three hours.

Thirty-eight minutes.

CHAPTER 2

I stood on my parents' balcony and watched the sun sink behind the Olympic Mountains. Cars rushing down the nearby freeway sounded like rolling waves: ebbing, flowing and whooshing like water instead of wheels and engines. The double-paned glass behind me was almost enough to drown out the chatter of my parents and siblings, but like the noise of the city, it was still there, humming at the edge of my consciousness the way the buzz of a tattoo needle did when I was at work.

Even with all the noise, this little pocket of the universe was still and quiet.

The mood was light here at la Casa de Wakefield as we celebrated my eldest sister's thirtieth birthday, but my heart wasn't in it, so I'd slipped out for a few minutes to get some air. Some *fresh* air, I'd assured my skeptical mother when she'd raised an eyebrow at me.

Her concern wasn't without merit. I was four months into my seventh, and so far most successful, attempt to quit smoking. I'd even started believing this might be it, that I'd given up nicotine for good, but the siren's call of a cigarette was almost irresistible tonight. It hadn't even crossed my mind to need one until hours after Luke had left my shop yesterday.

When the craving did come, though, it came on strong. Fortunately, I had neither smokes nor a lighter with me, so I just watched the sun go down and pretended I wasn't itching for just one tiny drag.

Behind me, the sliding glass door hissed open, letting all the voices from inside slip out into the stillness. Then it clicked shut, and the voices were cut off, leaving me with the river of cars, the muffled chatter, and the scuff of someone else's footsteps behind me.

I didn't have to ask who it was. More than that, I didn't have to ask why he was out here, and I wanted to groan with frustration. My mouth watered even before he confirmed my suspicion with the *smack, smack, smack* of the pack against his wrist. Cellophane tore. Paper crinkled. Blood pounded in my ears.

My dad appeared beside me, and I turned to him just in time to see him pull a delicious, unlit cigarette from the newly opened pack.

With the cigarette halfway to his mouth, he froze. "Oh, crap. Sorry, son." He started to put it back in the pack. "Didn't even think about it."

I gestured dismissively. "No, it's okay. Go ahead."

"You sure? I can go down to the garage if—"

"No, no, it's fine." I forced a laugh. "I have to get used to it eventually."

He hesitated, then shrugged and lifted the cigarette to his mouth. He cupped his hand around the end and held up the lighter with the other. The lighter clicked, and an orange flame flickered to life, reflecting on his face.

When he went to take that first glorious drag, I looked

away. I focused my attention on the city. On anything but the cigarette I so desperately wanted. He blew out a breath, and I knew he'd turned so he wouldn't blow it in my face, but the smell made it to me anyway.

"You all right tonight, son?" he asked.

I nodded, still staring out at the glowing ashes of the sunset and the smoky clouds swirling around the darkening edges of the smoldering horizon.

"You sure?"

Another nod, and he pressed no further. The quiet hiss of another drag made me shiver. I tapped my fingers on the railing. *God, why am I craving a smoke so badly?* It had been two months since I'd had to fight more than the most fleeting temptation, but tonight, it was almost as unbearable as it had been the first two or three days. *Why now? Why—*

Oh. Right.

Luke and his damned tattoo.

I exhaled hard, closing my eyes and pinching the bridge of my nose.

"You sure you're okay with me smoking out here?" Dad asked. "I can put it out, you know."

"It's not the smoke." I rested my hand on the railing again. "I think I just want one because my nerves are fucking shot right now."

"Oh?" He tapped his cigarette in the ashtray. "What's going on?"

I swallowed. "You'll never guess who showed up at the shop yesterday."

"The health department inspector?"

I shot him a good-natured glare. "Come on. You could eat off the floor in my shop."

He chuckled. "Okay, then who?"

"Luke." His name tasted like bitter ashes.

Dad's cigarette stopped half an inch from his lips. "Luke? As in, your ex-boyfriend?"

"The one and only."

He lowered his hand without taking a drag. "What the hell did he want?"

"A tattoo."

"From you?"

"Insisted on it," I muttered. "I tried to pawn him off on Jason, but..." I shook my head.

Dad finally took that last drag off the dying cigarette, then snuffed it out in the ashtray. "Seems a bit odd for him to just show up out of the blue and expect you to tattoo him."

"I know." I watched the thin tendril of smoke rising from the cooling ashes. Then I looked out at the city and shook my head again. "I don't know what to make of it, honestly."

"Think he's just trying to mess with you?"

"I wouldn't put it past him." I laughed bitterly. "And if he is, he's doing a damned good job of it."

"Do you think he might be trying to make amends with you?"

I blinked. "By having me tattoo him?"

He shrugged. "Why not?"

"I could think of slightly less painful methods," I said. "Like, I don't know, apologizing."

"Maybe this is just his way of reconnecting with you so he *can* apologize."

"A phone call would have been more than sufficient."

"You could have hung up on him if he had."

I pursed my lips. That was exactly what I would have done, now that he mentioned it. Once the shock had worn off, anyway.

I cleared my throat. "Or he could have said it when he showed up at my shop." I ran a hand through my hair and sighed. "That, and why would he suddenly want to make amends after all this time?"

"Does everything that happened still bother you?"

"Of course it does."

"Well, maybe it's been bothering him too."

"Is four years enough time to grow a conscience?"

Dad laughed. "I don't know about that, but it's certainly enough time to mature enough to see the mistakes of the past more clearly."

I said nothing. The mistakes of *my* past had certainly become more apparent in the last twenty-four hours. "I doubt he's changed."

"What if he has?"

I eyed him, then laughed. "That'll be the day."

Dad shrugged. "I'm serious. You guys were both kids when all of this went down. You've changed a lot since then. Maybe he has too."

My laughter faded. "I don't know. I mean, okay, we were young, but we weren't *that* young."

He raised an eyebrow. "Twenty-one *is* that young, Sebastian. It's like sixteen except you can legally drink." He gave me a pointed look. "And if I recall, the two of you did more than your fair share of that."

My face burned a little. "Okay, but even when I was so drunk I couldn't see straight, I never cheated on him."

"But you did plenty of stupid shit, no?"

I dropped my gaze, then sighed and nodded. "Yeah. I did."

"And were you always drunk when you did stupid shit?"

I managed a quiet laugh. "God, no."

"Okay, and you're a little older now, a hell of a lot wiser, and probably wouldn't do any of it again." He paused. "Well, most of it."

I laughed again. "Point taken."

"So, what makes you think he hasn't changed when you have?"

I swallowed hard. "Dad, even if he has changed, there are some things I never would have considered doing back then." I bit my lip for a second. "I never did anything to hurt him. I've never gone out of my way to hurt anyone. Even in my drunkest, darkest, stupidest moments, I've never deliberately done something to hurt someone, particularly not someone I loved."

"I know." He nodded slowly. "You've caused your fair share of trouble, but you've always had a good heart. For that matter, so did he, even if he didn't always behave that way."

"I have to wonder about him," I muttered.

"Do you think he was really out to hurt you?"

"He certainly wasn't making much of an effort not to, and—" I paused. "Wait, am I hearing you right? Because I swear you sound like you're defending him."

Dad shrugged again. "Son, he worked you over. Big time. You were better off without him when he left you."

"But...?"

"But, I can't help thinking if he's suddenly showing up after all these years, then maybe it's at least worth listening to whatever it is he has to say."

"Somehow I doubt that."

"Let me ask you this." He shifted his weight and leaned forward, resting his forearms on the railing. "Would you let just anyone ink you?"

"No way."

"And if you knew a particular artist hated you and would be sorely tempted to botch your tattoo just for spite, would you let him anywhere near you with a needle?"

I watched my fingers drum on the railing. "Of course not."

"Seb, for all his faults, Luke is not an idiot." Dad pushed himself up off the railing and shrugged almost apologetically. "I can't help wondering if this isn't some way of showing you he trusts you."

I snorted. "Why shouldn't he trust me? I'm not the one who cheated."

"No, but he's putting his skin and a tattoo that obviously means a lot to him in your hands," he said. "Which tells me that he either thinks *really* highly of you as a tattoo artist, or he's sure, deep down, that you don't hate him enough to fuck it up."

"Or, being the smart man you evidently think he is, he knows I wouldn't risk my professional reputation by botching a tattoo."

"Fair enough," he said. "But knowing him, if he's showing up after all this time, there's more to it than just wanting to mess with your head this way."

I reached up to rub the back of my neck. "Maybe you're right. I'm just not sure I want to hear what he has to say."

"You never know."

It's Luke, Dad. I know. I think I know.

I looked at him. "I guess I'll see what happens."

"About all you can do." He took a deep breath, then released it. "Listen, I know it's not easy to see someone like him after all this time, and maybe I'm just an eternal optimist, but I do think people can change."

"You have more faith in some people than I do, I guess," I said, almost whispering.

"Sebastian, let me tell you something. I've watched my oldest kid go from a drug-dealing, teenaged mother into the responsible, hard-working woman your sister is today. I've watched my second barely graduate high school, nearly wind up in jail more times than I can count, and then turn around, pull himself up by the bootstraps, and get his ass married and into medical school." He clapped my shoulder. "And I've watched my youngest do some stupid, *stupid* things over the years, only to turn into someone I'm just as proud of as my other children. If the three of you can get your shit together, then I have faith that Luke can grow up too."

I swallowed hard, avoiding my father's eyes.

"Do you understand what I'm saying, son?"

"Yeah, I understand."

"I could be totally wrong," he said. "Luke could still be the same dipshit I wanted to drop-kick off the twelfth floor. But I could be right."

I nodded but said nothing.

"Just give him the benefit of the doubt. You never know." He clapped my shoulder again. "Now let's get back in there and be social before your mother thinks I'm sneaking you cigarettes again."

I laughed, and we headed back into my parents' condo. As Dad closed the sliding glass door behind us, I stole a glance at my watch.

One day.

Twenty-one hours.

Thirteen minutes.

And I still wanted a damned cigarette.

LATER THAT NIGHT, THERE WERE ANGELS ALL OVER MY

damned kitchen table. Everywhere, there were angels. I must have had fifteen or twenty of them spread across the table. Half-drawn, partially erased, barely outlined, completely shaded, and still I hadn't quite gotten any of them right.

I chewed the end of my pen and glared at the latest version, which was as close as I'd gotten so far to the image in my head. I rubbed my eyes. It never took me this long to get a design right, particularly not when I had an original to go by. It shouldn't have taken this much work to modify a damned angel, add some lettering and call it a day.

Then again, being able to concentrate might have helped, and that wasn't happening. I shook my head, muttered a few obscenities under my breath and continued with the current design.

It was funny. Drawing, particularly tattoos, was my escape from the rest of the world. This headspace was where I went when I needed to get away from everything else. Even though it was what I did for a living, it was still a sacred mental oasis.

Luke had invaded that oasis. He was the reason for the lines and shadows on the paper in front of me, and he occupied my thoughts whether I concentrated on the drawing or thought about his visit.

From another time and place, I heard Luke's voice: "Drawing instead of studying again?"

I'd looked up from a sketch—a pair of tree frogs for a friend, if I remembered right—and he'd grinned as he pulled up a chair at the kitchen table.

I laid my pen beside the half-finished tree frogs and leaned back in my chair. "I still have time to study."

He chuckled. "Uh-huh, heard that before."

"You're not studying, either, so you're one to talk."

"That's because I finished two hours ago."

I groaned. "Fucking overachiever."

Luke laughed. "Hardly. I just have an easy course load this quarter."

"Must be nice."

"It is," he said. "But next quarter's going to suck. Looks like I'll be taking physics, which is not my best subject."

I grimaced. "You're on your own with that one. Chemistry, I can help. Physics? Sorry."

"You're a big help." He gestured at the design in front of me. "So, what are you working on?"

I shrugged. "It's not done yet."

"No shit. Otherwise you wouldn't still be working on it." He beckoned with two fingers. "Come on, let me see it."

I sighed and slid it across the table, cringing inwardly as he picked it up. I knew I was good, but now that I was on the road toward calling myself a professional, I doubted every line I drew.

Luke looked at me and smiled. "This is really, really good, Seb." He slid it back across the table. "I don't know how you do it."

My cheeks burned. "Thanks." I tapped the end of my pen on the drawing. "Now, if drawing frogs and Celtic knots would get me a passing grade in Shakespearean Lit, I'd be in good shape."

"With the talent you have for this, you don't *need* a passing grade in Shakespearean Lit." He rose and went to the refrigerator. "Beer?"

I sighed. "Much as I'd love one, I really should get to studying at some point tonight."

"Beer's always good for that."

"Maybe for you." I closed my eyes and rubbed the back of my stiff neck with both hands. "Once I have one, the last thing I'm going to want is to even think of *Julius Caesar*."

"Oh? And what will you want to think of?"

I eyed him, trying unsuccessfully not to grin at the mischievousness in his eyes. "What do you think?"

He raised his beer in a mock toast. "Finish your homework, and I'll show you."

"Great, now I'll never be able to concentrate."

He just laughed.

"If I were a dishonest man, I'd have you write the paper for me." I cocked my head. "How the hell do you get so into Shakespeare, anyway? It damn near puts me into a coma."

He chuckled. "It's all in how you read it." He set an unopened bottle of Budweiser in front of me and put his hands on my shoulders. He squeezed gently, kneading the muscles until they relaxed at his command. "Take Octavius in the last act of *Julius Caesar*." He kneaded a little harder, and God only knew how I managed to focus on his voice when he spoke again. "*Let us treat him in accordance with his virtue, with all respect and rites of burial.*" He leaned down and whispered in my ear, in the most flirtatious tone he could muster, "*His bones shall lie within* my *tent tonight.*"

I snorted with laughter. "Only you would find something dirty in that line.

"I passed the class, didn't I?" He kissed my cheek and stood, but didn't let go of my shoulders. He kept massaging out tension I didn't even know existed. Even when the knots were gone and the stiffness had long since left my neck, he didn't stop.

I groaned softly and let my head fall forward. "If you keep doing that, I'm not going to get any studying done tonight."

"Oh? What a shame."

He kept doing that.

I didn't get any studying done that night.

Looking over the latest incarnation of A.J.'s angel, I shivered at the memory. It was a wonder Luke and I ever got anything done when we lived together, and it was no surprise I wasn't making much progress tonight.

I reached for my Coke can, but it was empty, so I got up and went to the refrigerator for another. After I'd opened the new can, habit had me absently heading for the sliding glass door and reaching into my back pocket with my free hand.

I stopped. I didn't have any cigarettes. I wasn't going to go get any cigarettes. The craving would go away, just as it always did.

The unfinished drawing on the table, however, wouldn't go away until I got it right and finished it. With a sigh of resignation, I sat again, picked up my pen and went to work.

It was after one in the morning before I finally finished and settled on three drawings. In the morning, I'd convert them to stencils at the shop and they'd be ready for Luke's appointment.

One version was basically the original with some added color. One was more stylized, with the angel's legs bent a little more and her wings curving to complement the contours of his arm—not that I knew them by heart—plus I'd made her hair longer to make the whole composition more pleasing to the eye. The third had the same changes, but I'd also adjusted her flat, unemotional facial expression to add a bit more life to her. Hopefully one of the three would be acceptable. The sooner he agreed to a stencil, the sooner I'd get the tattoo started and finished. The sooner he'd be out of my shop and out of my life where he belonged.

I put the final drawings into a folder and glanced at the clock with exhausted eyes.

One day.

Seventeen hours.

Forty-six minutes.

CHAPTER 3

I'VE OFTEN HEARD THAT STARING AT A CLOCK ONLY makes the time go slower. Much like a watched pot never boils, a constantly monitored clock will always stay just shy of *that* time. Whatever time. Quitting time, party time, lunch hour, witching hour.

Watching the skinny red arms blur past oversized black numbers on a no-brakes collision course with seven o'clock, I decided that little theory was a heap of bullshit.

Every tattoo made the time fly. I hung on to every second of downtime I could get, staring at the clock and trying to draw the day out as long as I could. Just my luck, though, I'd had three walk-ins today, all of which made the time go by even faster. I was half-tempted to go renew my driver's license a few months early, figuring sitting in line at the Department of Licensing would slow the sands of the hourglass to a more sensible trickle.

Before I knew it, I'd bandaged up a high-powered lawyer's barbed-wire-and-roses tramp stamp, sent her on her way, and found myself staring down my own chicken-scratched *L. Emerson* in the appointment book.

Twenty-six minutes.

Forty-five seconds.

Heart pounding, I took a deep breath and looked over the three possible stencils for Luke's tattoo. I had also printed the initials in several different sizes and fonts to see what he preferred. As I went through them, I wondered who A.J. was. Had he been a lover? Maybe just a friend? I couldn't think of any relatives who'd gone by that name, though Luke had been close to a cousin named Aidan. The American flag suggested A.J. was in the military. Quite possibly a casualty of one of the wars. God knew I'd done plenty of memorial tattoos for fallen soldiers.

I slipped the stencils into a folder and set it beside my workstation. As I set everything up—gloves, brand new sets of needles, freshly cleaned machine and a few million other necessities—my heart beat faster. I hadn't been this nervous about tattooing someone since the very first time I put a needle to someone's skin. My hands shook as I arranged the various colors of ink, pouring a little of each into small plastic cups.

I need a drink. I need a smoke. I need someone else to do this fucking tattoo.

My mind echoed with my dad's advice to just hear Luke out and see what, if anything, he had to say. I hoped he was just here for a tattoo and, once his skin was bandaged and burning, would ride off into the sunset.

I hoped, but in the back of my mind, I was curious. Why now? Was my dad on to something when he suggested there was more to this than Luke's preference for me as an artist? I was good at what I did, and I made no apologies for saying so, but I could have named at least a dozen artists in the area who were as good or better than me. Hell, the woman who'd taught me was still practicing just four miles away in a shop that had more plaques and trophies on the walls than tattoo designs.

But he'd come to me. And any minute, he'd—

Behind me, the bell above the door jingled. I cringed.

"Can I—oh, you're here for the seven o'clock, aren't you?" Jason said.

"Yes. Luke Emerson." Three words, and each in turn hit my system like I'd just taken a massive drag off my first cigarette in ages. My head spun and my hands shook, but I gritted my teeth and forced myself to focus on getting ready for my client. Not Luke, not the ex-boyfriend I'd rather choke than tattoo—my *client*.

"Seb, you ready for him?" Jason asked.

Now there's a loaded question.

"Just about," I threw over my shoulder. "Would you mind having him sign the waiver and everything while I finish getting ready?"

"Not a problem."

Voices murmured and papers shuffled behind me. Jason ran him through the basic gist of our waiver, which essentially said that if I royally fucked up his tattoo, or if it got infected or something, he couldn't hold me or the shop liable unless there was evidence of criminal negligence. I chuckled to myself at the images my very, very dark sense of humor sent through my mind. I would never dream of actually doing any of it, but it was still entertaining to imagine "accidentally" carving *Unrepentant Whore* into his skin.

The folder with the stencils in it caught my eye, and I remembered he hadn't yet settled on a final design. I picked it up and went to the counter, pretending his very presence, his rapidly increasing nearness, didn't make me light-headed. That he didn't make me dizzy with—

Anger. Bitterness. Pure, unfiltered loathing.

Nothing more. Nothing less.

I met his eyes briefly as I slid the folder across the counter. "I played around with the design a little. Let me know which you want to use, or if you want me to make any more changes."

He flipped the folder open as I turned to finish setting up.

"There are also some different fonts in there," I said. "And some different sizes."

"So I see. These are—" Luke's breath caught. "Seb..."

I turned around, eyebrows raised. He held up one of the stencils, lips parted as he stared at it.

"What's wrong?" I asked.

"Nothing," he breathed. His eyes flicked toward me. "This one." He gestured with the stencil. "This is perfect. Absolutely perfect."

I took it from him. It was the stylized version with the longer hair, more expressive face, and curved wings. I nodded and set it beside my workstation.

"What about the lettering?"

He shuffled through a few different versions, finally settling on one that was a script font, but was fairly simple rather than ostentatious. With stencils agreed upon and organized, I gestured for him to come back behind the counter.

"Have a seat." I nodded toward my workstation.

The leather chair squeaked as he got comfortable, and I resisted the urge to shudder. So, here we were. We were really doing this. Making sure my back was to him, I closed my eyes and took a deep breath. No matter how much I wanted to choke him just for breathing, I had to relax and be civil. I couldn't tattoo while I was tense or angry.

Or turned-on.

Which was absolutely not a risk with Luke in the room.

Jason came out of the back, pulling on his leather jacket. My pulse jumped. *Tell me you're not leaving already...*

"Hey, I have to run out of here," he said. "Kimber's making some more arrangements tonight, and I need to go make sure she doesn't go over budget again."

I laughed. "No rest for the engaged, eh?" *You bastard. I hope she's picked the most expensive photographer in Seattle.*

"Pretty much." Zipping his jacket, he glanced at Luke, then at me. "You have everything under control here?"

"I'll call you if I burn the place down."

He chuckled. "Whatever. Have a good night, man."

"You too."

He picked up his motorcycle helmet from behind his workstation and headed for the door. Once again, the bells above the door preceded a massive spike in my blood pressure. I was seriously considering removing those things. They always seemed to signal that I had nerve-racking company or was suddenly alone.

Alone with Luke Emerson.

Focus. Time to be Sebastian the Tattooist, not Sebastian the Bitter Ex-boyfriend.

I sat beside him in my own chair. That was when I realized he'd worn a button down shirt. The sleeve would roll easily to his elbow, but to the shoulder? Not a chance. Even if it did, it would likely be too tight to keep that way for any length of time. If it wasn't too tight, we ran the risk of having it fall and screw up my work.

"You'll want to, um." I paused, swallowing hard. "Take your shirt off."

"Oh. Right." He sat up, and I looked anywhere but right at him while he unbuttoned his shirt. Fabric rustled, leather squeaked, and he announced he'd finished partially disrobing by saying, "Where should I put this?"

I can think of at least one place.

I coughed to mask a laugh that nearly escaped. "I'll take it." He handed me his shirt, and only then did I steal a glance at him. Thankfully, he'd worn a T-shirt underneath. Those sleeves were easier to secure than a rolled-up long sleeve, and the rest of the shirt kept his chest and abs safely out of sight. Well, as out of sight as washboard abs could be when covered by a T-shirt that was *that* tight.

You son of a bitch.

Our eyes met briefly. We both quickly shifted our gazes away. I had no doubt the rush of heat in my face had turned my cheeks a nice shade of pink, and I couldn't decide if his quiet chuckle was from nerves or if it was a smug acknowledgment that he'd caught me checking him out.

I forced myself not to look at him except for the skin I was being paid to mutilate. Pushing aside all of my impure and unprofessional thoughts, I concentrated on prepping him for the tattoo. I ran a disposable razor over his upper arm, making sure even the tiniest hairs were out of the way. Then I cleaned his skin and put the stencil on it, transferring the temporary ink to give me a guideline.

I sat back and scrutinized the lines. Gesturing at the mirror on the other side of the room, I said, "Have a look. Make sure it's straight and exactly where you want it to be."

He got up and went to the mirror. For a moment, he inspected the outline. He reached for it as if he wanted to run his fingers over it, but wisely hesitated before smearing the ink. His expression was almost reverent, and for the millionth time, I wondered just who A.J. was.

He must have been someone special, I thought, and that tightness in my chest had nothing to do with jealousy.

Jealousy. Jesus. The very thought of being jealous of A.J. was both petty and pathetic. The man had died, for God's sake. Whoever he was, he was gone now, and obviously he'd meant something to the man who'd repeatedly treated me like a doormat for his revolving door.

Anger swelled in my chest, but I took a deep breath and reminded myself to be professional. No sense getting worked up over the past. Relax, be civil and just get through this. Then it would be over and he'd be gone. Forever. I hoped.

I cleared my throat. "How does it look?"

Barely whispering, he said, "Perfect."

"Ready, then?"

He took one last glance in the mirror, then nodded and returned to the chair. Once he was comfortable, I picked up the needle. He eyed it warily as I moved it toward his skin.

"This is just going to be the needle," I said. "No ink. To make sure you can tolerate the pain."

He swallowed. "Is it really that bad?"

"You tell me." *Not like it's the first prick you've ever felt.* I bit my tongue to keep from laughing.

Then I pressed the pedal down, and Luke shivered when the needle buzzed to life. Using my right thumb and forefinger to keep his skin tight, I touched the needle to him with my left. Just like everyone did, he sucked in a hiss of breath and every muscle in his body tensed, but he didn't jerk his arm away, nor did he freak out.

"How does that feel?" I asked.

"It fucking tickles," he muttered.

I laughed. Typical response. "So you can handle an hour and a half of that?"

He took a breath, then nodded.

I dipped the needle in a cup of black ink. "Here we go, then."

At first, just like most people, he tensed every time the needle touched him. With every line, though, he relaxed a little more. If the endorphins hadn't kicked in yet, they would soon. Some people were in pain right to the end; others sailed away on an endorphin high, especially if the tattoo was in a highly sensitive area. Still others winced and flinched the whole time, but with progressively less enthusiasm as they got used to it.

For a long time, we didn't speak. I concentrated on the lines. He probably tried to think of anything but what I was doing.

All the while, I couldn't shake that unsettled feeling, the same feeling I'd had since he'd walked into the shop the other day. There were things that needed to be said. What, I didn't know, but there was something. If, as my father had suggested, Luke was here to talk to me, he wasn't being very forthcoming about it. Though I supposed he might not have predicted just how intense the pain would be. That burn was something to which I'd long become accustomed, but it hurt. It definitely hurt. Whatever speech he'd intended to give was probably stuck behind his tightly clenched teeth.

Or maybe he knew that whatever he had to say would elicit an emotional reaction from me. Perhaps from both of us. As my dad had said, Luke wasn't stupid, and maybe he'd thought twice about pissing me off while I was already inflicting pain on him.

I was of two minds. Get it out and get it over with? Or just quietly proceed with my work and hope this was the end of it? Either way, this was going to be one of the most difficult tattoos of my career, simply because I couldn't fucking concentrate.

If it wasn't the unspoken or the unknown, it was his physical presence. The very fact that he was here. In my shop. In a muscle-tight T-shirt stretched over *those* abs and *those* shoulders. Thick, medical grade gloves kept me from touching his skin, but they might as well have been made of the same ultra-thin latex as some of the newer, barely there condoms for all they did to keep his body heat from reaching my nerve endings.

As much as it killed me to admit it to myself, I couldn't deny I was still attracted to him. Physically, anyway. He had an amazing body, and I had the misfortune of knowing exactly what that body was capable of. For all he'd hurt me back then, I'd have been lying to myself if I tried to say our sex life had been anything but spectacular. We had knee-trembling quickies whenever and wherever we could. We burned the midnight oil making love, even if it was just kissing and touching, for hours. It could be a single candle, Fourth of July fireworks, or anything in between. If anyone ever asked me to name the hottest sexual moment of my life—or wildest, most sensual, most daring, most emotional, whatever—I could guarantee it involved Luke.

With him right here in front of me, with my hands on him, the thought of spending just one night with him was tempting. So, so tempting. One night without all the bull-shit, without—

It's over, Seb. It's in the past.

I dipped the needle in a cup of water to rinse it while I shook my head to clear my thoughts. That sex life was a past life, and that's how it needed to stay. Eventually, my body would get that message.

Before I put the needle on his arm again, I stopped to watch his face. His eyes were tightly closed, his lips pressed together in a thin, bleached line. Even without the needle touching him, he didn't release his breath.

"Luke, breathe."

He let out a long breath. Inhaled again. Held it.

Great. He was one of *those* clients, the kind who focused so hard on the tattoo and the pain, they forgot to breathe. If my experience had taught me anything, there was only one thing that could distract a person like this enough to keep them breathing: conversation.

I gritted my teeth. Letting him pass out from lack of air sounded awfully tempting just then, but my professional, safety-conscious side won.

"So, um, what have you been doing these days?" *Why are you here?*

He jumped as if the sound of my voice had startled him. Then he muffled a cough with his free hand. "Just, you know, working. I've been—*Jesus.*"

"Sorry. That spot's sensitive on a lot of people." The edges of the angel's wings curled around toward the back of his arm, which could be quite tender. "I'll be done with this part in a minute. Anyway, go on." *Why now, Luke?*

He took and released a deep breath. "I've been working on my master's in between, well, working."

I dipped the needle and glanced up at him. "Your master's?" *Who was A.J.?*

He nodded. "MBA."

"Oh." I continued with the line I was working on. "Sounds...ambitious." *I don't understand why you're here.*

"Well, a bachelor's wasn't getting me quite the paycheck I wanted, so it seemed like a good idea."

"Does it still seem like a good idea?" *What makes you think* this *was a good idea?*

He chuckled. "I sometimes wonder." His laughter turned into another sharp breath.

"I'm almost done with this part." *Tell me why the fuck you're here.* "Just keep breathing."

"Easy for you to say," he said through clenched teeth.

"Hey, mine goes all the way around. I *know* what it feels like."

He turned his head toward me. "So, the sleeves," he said, furrowing his brow as he looked at the tattoos on my arms. "Do they go all the way to your shoulders?"

Touching my shirt with only a paper towel, I brought my T-shirt sleeve up enough to reveal that the ink did in fact extend from my wrist to my shoulder.

"Wow," he said. "They're...I really like them."

"Thanks." I managed a genuine, if weak, smile. I gestured at my right forearm, which was still bare in a few places. "I'm still working on this one."

He laughed quietly. "I still can't figure out how you tattoo yourself."

"Practice," I said with a shrug.

"Yeah, but it—" He flinched. "But it fucking hurts."

I chuckled. "You get used to it."

"I'm sure." He craned his neck slightly. "How does mine look so far?"

"It'll be better when it's done." I leaned in a little, focusing on the ends of the angel's hair. "Just so you know, it won't be pretty for a few days. Between the swelling and the scabbing, don't freak if it's not what you want right away."

He laughed softly. "I know. I remember."

My eyes flicked up and met his. My cheeks burned, his darkened a little, and we both looked away. There it was. The subtle acknowledgment that we had a past, a past that wouldn't be forgotten. Not to mention all the unasked, unanswered questions about what the hell we were doing in the present. Minute by minute it became clearer that we would only get away with this artist-client charade for so long.

That didn't mean we couldn't at least try to keep it going, though.

"So," he said, "what do you do if you make a mistake?"

"Cross it out and start over."

"Very funny."

I chuckled. "It's not that hard to fix unless I really fuck it up."

"Ever really screwed one up?"

I dipped the needle and glanced up at him before putting it back to his skin. "Never anything that required laser surgery to fix, but I've had to get creative a time or two to cover something up."

"Ever misspelled one?"

I laughed. "No. I'm way too paranoid about that." I furrowed my brow as I worked on the angel's hands, which were a particularly intricate area of the design. "I did hit a nerve once and have a client jerk so hard it jacked up an area I was shading."

"How much did it take to fix that?"

I shrugged. "It wasn't too difficult, but it was a bit painful for her though, since the needle dug in pretty hard."

"Ouch."

"Yeah." I looked over the tattoo. Most of the outline was complete. It was an intricate design, so it would take this appointment to get all of the edges, along with some very basic shading and details. Next time, I'd go through and shade the whole thing. Tonight, the only thing left was...

Something sank in my gut.

The lettering.

Two letters, two periods and a thousand hidden questions.

I rinsed the needle, dipped it into the ink and started on the second period. I always started lettering on the right and worked my way backwards to the first letter. Since I was left-handed, it was a habit left over from drawing and painting. Kept me from dragging my hand through what I'd already done. It occasionally resulted in a partially smeared stencil, but I preferred doing that to resting my hand in raw, freshly tattooed skin.

As I worked, I couldn't help thinking about the man whose name I slowly etched into Luke's arm.

Who are you, A.J.?

Luke released a hiss of breath as I started on the J. He pulled in another, and I wasn't surprised when he didn't let it go. I knew I needed to keep him talking, but I was afraid of where I might take the conversation if I spoke again. I was almost done, so I silently pleaded with him to hang in there. And even as I did, my thoughts drifted to A.J.

What mark did your life leave on his that meant your death should mark his skin?

Dipping the needle once more, I looked at the lettering. The angel. The redness of Luke's skin as it responded to the minor trauma I'd inflicted. The grimace on his lips as he gingerly drew a breath.

Would he have done this if something had ever happened to me?

No, I wouldn't think about that. I focused as hard as I could on the lettering, thinking only about lines and dots, ignoring the sum to which all those lines and dots added up. Ignoring Luke. Ignoring this unnerving proximity to the only man who'd ever fucked me so good and hurt me so bad.

After a while, I leaned back and checked over my handiwork. The lettering was done.

"That's enough for tonight." I took my foot off the pedal, and the buzzing died, leaving us in silence. I gestured with the needle at the mirror. "It's completely outlined, and I'll do all of the shading next time. Go have a look, let me know what you think."

He stood, pausing to twist a crick out of his back and roll some stiffness out of his arm and shoulder. When he got to the mirror, I watched his expression as he took in the partially finished design. A nostalgic smile crossed his face, and if the distant look in his eyes was any indication, he'd all but forgotten I was here.

"Does it look okay?" I asked.

He jumped. Yep, he'd forgotten, if only for a moment, that I was here. I wasn't quite sure how I felt about that.

"It's great." He faced me. "Thank you, Seb. It's incredible. Better than I expected."

"You're welcome," I murmured. I held his gaze for a moment, then dropped mine. "Well, let me put a bandage over it, and then you can be on your way."

He started toward the chair, but I stopped him.

"Go ahead and stay standing. I need to get up and move myself." I stood, pausing as he had done to twist the stiffness out of my hips and back. Then I picked up the bandage and tape. "Hold still for a second."

As I gently taped the bandage over the tattoo, I couldn't help thinking about how long it had been since I'd stood this close to him. He was a few inches taller than me, and our height difference had always given me the perfect vantage point to kiss his neck. My God, he'd loved that. He'd never tired of it, nor had I tired of doing it, and we could go on that way for hours at a time. There were so many deliciously erogenous zones between his jaw and his collar-bones, and I knew them so well, I could have tattooed a map highlighting every last one of them. Same with the entire length of his spine. And the inside of his thigh.

I cleared my throat as I put the last piece of tape into place. "There, that should—"

I looked up, and we both froze.

He'd craned his neck to inspect the bandage, and when our eyes met, our faces were close. So. Damned. Close. I probably could have smelled his cologne just then if I'd been able to breathe at all.

He swallowed hard. Before I could stop myself, I watched the ripple run down the front of his throat. My mouth watered as I remembered tasting his lightly stubbled skin. The way his voice vibrated against my lips when he moaned the way he always did whenever I found one of those secret erogenous zones. The way his whole body would shudder when I nipped the place where his neck met his shoulder. There are some things a man just doesn't forget in four years.

Like how much it hurt when it was over.

Reality washed over me like cold water, and I broke eye contact, releasing his arm and stepping back, nearly shoving him away in the process.

"Anyway," I said quickly, "that's it. For now. Just—" I hesitated. A million times I'd given the instructions for caring for a new tattoo, and tonight, they were lost on me.

He took the clips off his T-shirt sleeve and carefully pulled it over the bandaged tattoo. I handed him his shirt, and we avoided looking at each other. While he put on his shirt, I took off my gloves and dug out a card detailing the instructions that, for the life of me, I couldn't recall.

We exchanged the card without speaking or touching.

Then he reached for his jacket and, as he put it on, grimaced and drew in a sharp breath that prompted the professional in me to remember I was still on the job.

"How's the pain?" I asked.

"Not too bad." He zipped his jacket halfway, then put his hands in the pockets. Then he jumped as if something had shocked him. "Shit, money. I almost forgot." He laughed softly and pulled out his wallet. "I guess I still have to pay you, don't I?"

I forced a smile. "That would help, yes."

"Hundred and fifty now, hundred and fifty next time?"

"That's fine, yes." I didn't care if he paid it all at the next appointment. Normally I required two thirds up front and the rest on completion, but I just wanted this night done and over with.

He pulled out his wallet, counted out the money and handed it to me. Just as we'd done with the instruction card, we made the exchange without touching, without speaking and without looking at each other.

And that was that. The tattoo was as done as it was going to get tonight. It was bandaged. He'd redressed. Money and instructions had traded hands. All he had to do now was leave, and the sooner the better.

"Well," he said. "I guess I'll see you in two weeks."

"Yeah. Two weeks." Something sank in my gut. Relief, that was all it was. Nerves unraveling now that tonight was finally over. I swallowed hard. "I'll, um, see you then."

Our eyes met.

"Right." He nodded. "See you then."

We still haven't discussed why you're here. "Have a good night."

"Yeah, you too." He turned to go and started for the door.

Wait, stay here. Let's discuss this. There's a reason you came to me tonight.

He slowed his gait, nearly stopping.

No, Luke. Go. Please. Get out of here.

He must have thought better of whatever he was about to say, if anything, because he kept going. When he pushed the door open, I'd never been so relieved to hear those bells jingle.

But he stopped. He hesitated for a moment, eyes focused on the ground beneath his feet while he hovered in the doorway. Before I could ask what was on his mind—and I don't know that I had the courage to finish the question anyway—he looked at me.

"I think I'm going to go out for a drink." He paused. "Wilde's is calling to me tonight." A hint of a grin tugged at his lips, and a second later, he was gone, the bells echoing inside the cavernous and all but deserted tattoo shop.

CHAPTER 4

I STARED AT THE CLOSED DOOR FOR THE LONGEST TIME, watching the bells sway back and forth.

It wasn't explicitly an invitation, but I hadn't forgotten that look. That grin. It was the same grin that had always followed a seemingly mundane comment that he was getting into the shower or going to bed. It meant nothing if not *but you're welcome to join me.*

There was no doubt in my mind he was silently suggesting I join him for more than just a drink. Four years and a tattoo appointment after he'd played me, cheated on me and left me for some slut on the other side of town, he really had the nerve to invite me to one of the swankiest meat markets in the city. Like I'd be enough of an idiot to voluntarily put myself in his path. Like I'd willingly subject myself to a night of hot, sweaty sex with the only man who'd ever been able to make me come *that* hard *that* many times.

As if a look and a suggestion could make me seriously consider going up to my apartment, changing clothes, calling a cab and—

Jesus, Seb. What are you thinking?

I rubbed my eyes and sighed. I was thinking with my dick, of course. I could tell myself all day long that I would never touch him again if my life depended on it, but I knew better. If I knew I could have him for one night and one night only, I would.

I drummed my fingers on the counter. And why couldn't I have him for one night and one night only? At least it wouldn't be like his appointment. No longer a captive audience, no longer bound by professionalism, I could leave the club any time I wanted. Or I could leave with him, indulge in a few orgasms, then walk away tomorrow morning and leave him in my past where he belonged. Well, aside from his remaining tattoo appointment, during which I'd think and behave like a professional. Just as I had tonight.

I am losing my mind. No two ways about it. I have lost my fucking mind.

I didn't even realize I'd reached for my back pocket until my fingers found nothing. No pack of smokes, no lighter.

I groaned aloud. Willpower was not in my vocabulary tonight. Though with my cravings for either nicotine or Luke, what I probably needed was a healthy dose of *won't* power.

Closing my eyes, I gripped the edge of the counter and tried not to think about smoking. Or Luke. Or that first, dizzying drag. Or the way his kiss always made me lightheaded. The rush of nicotine hitting my system. The blinding, earth-shaking power of an orgasm.

I exhaled hard. I was backsliding on one broken addiction or the other tonight. It was either a cigarette or Luke Emerson. At this moment, I couldn't decide which was worse for my health. I knew for damn sure which tasted better, though.

Before I could talk myself out of it or convince myself a cigarette was the wiser of the two choices, I locked up the shop and walked across the street to my apartment.

On the cab ride to the last place in the universe I should have gone tonight, I chewed my thumbnail and stared out the window. This would be on my terms tonight. The last time we'd had sex, it had been under the illusion that we were still in love. I knew he'd cheated before, and I'd foolishly forgiven him far too many times, so I shouldn't have been surprised he was doing it again. Nor should I have been surprised that the next day, he was gone.

And tomorrow, I would be gone. I had no illusions about what tonight would be. This would be sex and nothing more. I'd enjoy it for what it was, get him out of my system once and for all, and go back to life as normal. As long as I didn't get emotionally tangled up with him again, I could do this and walk away unscathed. Well, mentally unscathed. Physically would be an entirely different story if Luke was the same lover he'd been back then.

The cab pulled up in front of Wilde's and lurched to a stop. While the driver ran my debit card, I looked at the club and chewed my lip. The pavement, wet from an afternoon rain, glittered red and yellow from the club's neon sign. There was no line outside the tinted glass doors, and the parking lot was only about half full, but it was still fairly early. In an hour or two, this place would be crowded with men on the prowl.

The driver handed me my debit card and a receipt. When I got out, my heart jumped into my throat. Was I really doing this? I very nearly turned around and got right back in, but the engine rumbled to life and the tires hissed across wet pavement.

Taking a deep breath, I started across the parking lot.

I hadn't been to Wilde's in a few weeks, but Casey the bouncer let me in without paying the cover. He'd known me for some time because my last boyfriend was a bartender here.

Dating a bartender definitely had its perks. The shift manager's boyfriend and I both got in here for nothing, and half our drinks were free too. Things with Kieran had ended amicably, and I still dropped in now and again to have a drink with him, so I still got in free. If I had a brain in my head, I'd be here tonight seeking out that ex, not the one with a fresh tattoo and dangerously tempting eyes.

As I walked up to the bar, Kieran's eyes lit up. "Hey, you. Good to see you."

"You too." I smiled and leaned across the bar to kiss him on the cheek. "How are things?"

He shrugged. "Not bad. Working my tail off, as always."

"Just don't work it all off." I tilted my head to conspicuously check out his ass, then winked at him.

"So, you've decided to slum it and show your face here again after all this time?" he asked with a good-natured glare.

I gave him a sheepish look. "Sorry. I've been busy."

He laughed. "Just giving you shit." He glanced around the club. "You came in on a good night. Crowd's still light, but the pickings are *hot*."

"Actually," I said, leaning on the bar and looking around, "I'm meeting someone."

His eyebrows jumped and he grinned. "Oh? Do tell."

"I'm not sure if he's here yet." I squinted, trying to pick out individual faces in the dim lighting. A few regulars, some familiar bartenders, plenty I'd never seen before, and—

There.

The hairs on the back of my neck stood on end, and now that I'd spotted him, there was no losing him in the crowd. His presence was simply...*here.* My heart pounded with a mixture of excitement and nervousness and arousal and *what the fuck am I doing here?*

I cleared my throat and gestured toward him. "The guy over there. Red shirt, black jacket."

Kieran leaned over the bar and looked in Luke's direction. "Ooh, very nice." We exchanged grins.

I looked at Luke again. Nerves coiled in the pit of my stomach. This was a mistake. This was dangerous. By showing up here, I'd tipped my hand. Told him, without saying a word, that our interaction didn't end at artist-client. I'd given the yes before the question was spoken.

I took a deep breath and tried to relax. Tonight would be on my terms, I reminded myself. I knew what he wanted, I knew what I wanted, and once we got what we both came for, that would be it.

"The usual?" Kieran's voice brought me out of my thoughts.

"Yes, thanks."

We exchanged smiles. If I really wanted to and he didn't already have plans tonight, I could probably persuade Kieran to come home with me after his shift. Wouldn't have been the first time. There were perks to dating bartenders, and there were perks to staying on friendly terms with exes. Free cover and free booze from the former, and the occasional night of no-strings-attached, no-bullshit sex from the latter.

"Kamikaze on the rocks." Kieran set the glass on a coaster and slid it toward me.

"Thanks," I said.

"Any time." Then he stepped away to take care of some other customers, but not before throwing a devilish grin over his shoulder. I knew that look as well as I knew the one Luke had given me earlier. The unspoken invitation.

Not tonight, I thought in spite of the pleasant shudder he sent rippling down my spine. Sex with Kieran was always hot, but I was in the mood to play with fire.

I shifted my attention back to Luke.

He'd moved, but my senses honed in on him without any difficulty. He was by the bar now, and he looked right back at me, lowering his chin in a parody of a nod. *Yes, I knew you'd be looking at me right then.*

I shifted my gaze to the dance floor. There were plenty of guys getting close there. Some kissing, some perilously close to it. A hand on someone's ass. Another under the back of a shirt. Fingers in someone's hair. A thick hard-on under tight jeans.

The dance floor and its occupants were the very picture of hot, but none of that drew my attention completely away from the intense, quiet presence beside the bar on the other side of the room.

He didn't come to me. I didn't go to him, and I had no intention of going to him. I'd come this far. I'd taken him up on this, and I was here. It was up to him to make the next move.

Especially since I didn't think I had the balls to do it.

We made eye contact again through the dim light. He watched me over the rim of his glass, and though I couldn't see his mouth, his eyes told me he was grinning. He took a long drink, then glanced down as he set his glass on the bar.

When our eyes met once more, he pushed himself away from the bar with his hip, and my pulse soared. I was certain he was heading this way, that he intended to close the crowded distance between us.

But he didn't.

He gave me one last glance, then disappeared into the crowd. Panic caught my breath in my throat. I lost him. My eyes darted back and forth, searching frantically. He hadn't gone far, but where was he?

There.

A flicker of movement drew my attention to the far corner of the room. He paused beneath the glowing green exit sign, waiting until I looked his way. As soon as I did, he disappeared down the hall by the restrooms and emergency exit.

I shouldered my way through the crowd, eyes fixed on that emergency exit sign like it was a damned beacon, as if I'd lose sight of it forever if I dared take my eyes off it. I wasn't losing sight of it, because I wasn't losing Luke. He'd turned this into a game of cat and mouse, and I couldn't decide if I was the predator pursuing or the prey being lured.

And truthfully, I didn't care, because every time my heart slammed against the inside of my ribcage, I was one second closer to tasting Luke.

The emergency exit was a few feet straight down the hallway. Just before that door, the hall made a sharp turn to the right, which was where the restrooms were. It was deserted back here, and the stark blue-green fluorescent lighting was dusk-dim, but almost blinding compared to the relative darkness of the rest of the club. I blinked a few times, and when my eyes had adjusted, I kept going.

I turned the corner and stopped.

The noise of the club faded behind the sound of my heartbeat, and even that nearly disappeared. Encased in the silence of this tiny hallway, Luke and I faced each other.

We weren't tattooist and client anymore. Not ex-boyfriends. The past, recent or otherwise, ceased to exist, and there was only now.

Only this.

Only us.

He took a step closer, the dull tap of his shoe echoing all around us.

The next step was mine.

Then his.

Inch by inch, never breaking eye contact or silence, we neared each other. When we were close enough to touch, I half-expected us to circle each other, as much like predators moving in for the kill as dancers falling into step.

No steps remained between us, only the sliver of space to be bridged by a touch. I couldn't breathe as Luke brought his hand up. Slowly, *slowly*, his fingers approached my face, gradually encroaching on my peripheral vision until their very nearness warmed my skin. His fingertips grazed my cheek, and I closed my eyes, releasing a ragged breath through parted lips. I'd spent an hour and a half with my hands on him earlier, touching him through gloves but touching him nonetheless, and that had been mostly —*strictly*—business.

Now it was anything but, and it showed. His touch was gentle and electric, awakening dormant nerve endings that existed only for Luke-fucking-Emerson.

"Look at me, Seb," he whispered, and his rum-tinged breath on my lips had the same effect as his fingers on my skin. "Look at me. Please."

I did, lifting my chin so I could look him in the eye.

Blood pounded in my ears. The hunger in his eyes mirrored my own, and I wondered if he was as painfully hard as I was.

Uncertainty crept into the back of my mind. *We can't do this. We shouldn't do this.* My stomach twisted and my chest tightened. All the bitterness and anger tried to make themselves known, but then his fingers combed through my hair, and I could barely stand or even breathe. *How am I supposed to hate you when I want you this badly?*

My fingers tingled with the need to feel the five o'clock shadow along his jaw, so I raised my hand, letting the pad of my thumb brush along the edge of his jaw. He shivered, closing his eyes for a second before looking down at me again. The tip of his tongue swept across his lower lip, and it was my turn to shiver.

We leaned in closer. Slowly. So, so slowly. I couldn't tell if it was caution, disbelief, or if we were both simply over-whelmed, but this predatory dance unfolded one glacial step at a time. When he breathed, the air between my lips moved, and it was only a matter of time before we touched.

The only thing more surreal than being this close to him after all this time was being so nervous, so unsteady. We'd fucked, we'd made love, we'd done anything and everything. I knew his body better than I knew my own, but this was different. I didn't know if we dared bring this long-dead thing back to life, even if only for one night, but could we stop if we tried?

His lip brushed mine, and that flash of gentle contact startled us apart. Only a fraction of an inch, but that was ground that had taken an absolute age to gain.

"Seb," he breathed, his voice unsteady, "I want you so fucking bad right now."

"I know." I gulped. When I spoke again, barely whispering as I stared into his intense blue eyes, my voice shook more than his had. "That's why I'm here."

"I'm..." Luke exhaled, releasing a long, warm breath against my lips that raised goose bumps along the entire length of my back. He drew another, and I thought he was about to speak again.

All at once, he seized the front of my jacket, slammed me up against the wall and instantly overwhelmed me. His desperate, demanding kiss. His hard cock against my own. Hands in my hair. His hair between my fingers. Stubble grazing stubble.

"Fucking Christ," he whispered, breaking the kiss and touching his forehead to mine. "You're..." His hands trembled in my hair. He pulled back a little, drawing away just enough to send panic surging through my veins. "Fuck. Seb, this is—"

"Kiss me again." *Don't you dare have second thoughts now.*

"What?"

"You heard me." I swallowed. "Just...kiss me again."

"Are you—"

I pulled him to me, and he must have forgotten whatever hesitation had crossed his mind because he kissed me deeply, passionately, pressing his erection against mine.

This kiss was no less violent than the first, but the shock had faded, and with the absence of *oh fuck, Luke's kissing me* occupying my thoughts, I finally tasted him.

Rum and Coke. Heavier on the rum than the Coke, just the way he'd always ordered it, and lingering lightly on his tongue as our mouths moved together. As the alcohol's flavor diminished, his kiss simply tasted like him. Like the baseline to which I'd compared every kiss I'd had since

Luke. Every man's kiss was warmer than, cooler than, gentler than, rougher than, sweeter than...*this*.

I pulled his hair back and bent to kiss his neck. Oh God, he still wore that cologne. Heady, spicy, with a hint of musk, along with that distinctive masculine scent that set off a million memories in my mind, every one of them different, every one of them *Luke*.

His voice vibrated the warm, coarsely stubbled skin against my lips, and it took a moment for the words to reach me through the delirium of all my other senses. When they did at last reach my ears and, eventually, my mind, I was damned thankful for the wall behind me because without it, I'd have sunk to the floor.

"Let's get out of here."

No more questions, spoken or otherwise. No turning back. My body needed him, and right or wrong, love him or hate him, tonight I would have him.

CHAPTER 5

WE GOT INTO A CAB AND LUKE GAVE HIS ADDRESS TO the driver. The whole way from Wilde's to Luke's, we neither spoke nor kissed. It wasn't lack of desire that kept us from continuing what we'd started in the hallway. Most of it had to do with the cab driver. Half politeness, half self-preservation. Even in Capitol Hill, Seattle's predominantly gay and gay-friendly neighborhood, we couldn't be sure how a driver would respond to two men making out in the backseat.

The driver aside, there was also the issue of restraint. I knew us. I knew myself. There was only so much either of us would be able to take before we forgot where we were or who else was around. Like no one else on God's green earth, Luke could make me forget myself. He was the only man I'd ever had the nerve to suck off in a movie theatre. I couldn't relax enough to do it with anyone else. With him, I must have done it a dozen times. Twice during one film.

So we didn't kiss, but we didn't stop touching, either.

I slid my hand up his thigh, letting my fingertips trail just below the inseam of his jeans. My breath caught when his did, and it was all I could do to stop a few inches shy of his cock. I wanted to touch him and tease him, but I didn't dare. Not here. Not now.

Luke slipped his hand into mine and drew light circles on the inside of my wrist with his thumb. He must have remembered the effect that had on me, and when I shivered, he laughed softly. Our eyes met.

The flicker of streetlights and headlights illuminated his face just enough to reveal the slight curl of his lips.

Goose bumps prickled my skin. *What else do you remember, Luke?*

He winked in the low light, and as if on cue, the cab slowed to a stop. We got out, and Luke paid the driver. A moment later, for the second time tonight, the hiss of tires on wet pavement left me somewhere I probably shouldn't have been.

On the way up the walk to his ground-level apartment, he snaked his arm around my waist, and it was all I could do to keep my feet under me.

"You okay?" he asked, releasing me to pull his keys out of his pocket.

I moistened my lips. "I will be in a few minutes."

His keys clanked on the pavement. He quickly scooped them up. Then he took the two porch steps at the same time, and I pretended not to notice the way his hands shook when he put the key in the lock. I pretended mine wouldn't have had the same problem had they not been balled into fists and jammed into my coat pockets.

Almost there. Almost there. Breathe.

He opened the door and I walked past him. I closed my eyes in the darkness of the hallway, taking a long, deep breath. I pulled my hands out of my pockets, opening and closing them just to give them something to do besides shake. It wasn't nerves now. No second thoughts, no hesitation. The lightning in my veins was pure, concentrated lust.

The deadbolt clicked into place behind me.

I gulped. My heartbeat shifted into overdrive.

I had just enough time to lift my heel off the floor, intending to turn around and face him, before his hands were on my hips. He kissed the side of my neck, and there was nothing gentle about it. His stubble scraped my skin and I half-expected him to sink his teeth in as he worked his way up to that sweet spot behind my ear.

Letting my head fall to the side to give him more access, I closed my eyes. "Jesus, Luke..."

His hand slid from my hip to the front of my jeans, and my back arched off his chest as he gently squeezed my erection. As if that sensation wasn't intense enough, he pulled my hips against him, making sure there was no mistaking he was just as hard as I was. My knees shook. I could barely breathe, not with his cock pressed against me like that. I couldn't remember the last time I'd wanted this badly to be thrown down and fucked. I couldn't remember the last time, but I'd have bet money it was with Luke.

His lip, or maybe just the warmth of his breath, brushed my skin. "Turn around."

As soon as I did, his mouth was against mine, and we were right back to that moment in the hallway at Wilde's. His tongue demanded access to mine. His fingers gripped my hair just tight enough to hurt. His cock—oh God, his thick, hard cock—pressed against mine.

Luke shifted his weight, pushing me back a step. Then another. I let him guide me down the hall, but between walking backwards and kissing him, I stumbled. Without thinking about it, I grabbed his arm for balance, but immediately let go when he released a grunt of pain.

"Sorry, sorry," I said. "I forgot about—"

"It's okay." He kissed me again and shoved my jacket off my shoulders. It fell to the floor behind me. God only knows how we stepped over it without falling on our asses, but with a little shuffling and wavering, we stayed on our feet.

I started to work off his jacket, but remembered his tattoo. Still kissing me, still guiding me one step at a time, Luke managed to shrug off his coat.

He reached past me and opened the door, then nudged me through it. The light came on. My shirt came off. As I tossed my shirt aside, Luke did a double take at my chest.

"That's new," he said. He watched his own fingers trail over all the ink that hadn't been there before. Then he grinned and met my eyes as he teased one of my nipple rings with his thumb and forefinger. "These are definitely new."

I bit my lip and let my head fall forward, the entire length of my spine threatening to liquefy when his free hand went for the other ring.

"Hmm, sensitive." He kissed the side of my neck again. "I'll remember that."

I moaned. He *would* remember, I knew he would, and he'd capitalize on it every chance he could.

I reached for his belt buckle, but between his lips on my neck and his fingers on my nipple rings, I couldn't quite remember how to work it.

"I've got a better idea." He let go and stepped back, hauling his shirt over his head before reaching for his half-unbuckled belt. I got the message and unbuckled my own belt. We both stripped out of our clothes as quickly as we could. I didn't look at him the whole time. I couldn't. Not if I had a prayer of getting all these clothes off, all these clothes, *fuck, why am I wearing so goddamned many clothes*?

I kicked my boxers out of the way and turned to face him.

Sweet mother of God.

He was just as toned and tanned as he'd ever been, with a thin dusting of dark hair across his broad, gorgeous chest. Below his spectacular abs, a narrow strip of that same dark hair extended from his navel down, drawing my attention straight to his cock.

Everything about him turned my brain and knees to water, and the latter was just as well because as soon as I was close to him again, I knelt so I could taste him.

The second my tongue made contact with his skin, I was in heaven. I could never get enough of the way his cock felt in my mouth. Soft skin pulled tight over his thick erection. All the ridges and contours that I could explore for hours if he let me. Hot, vaguely salty. His hands in my hair. His moans in the otherwise silent air around us.

I ran one hand up the side of his leg, partly to touch him and partly to stabilize myself. That was when I realized his knees shook too. His fingers drew unsteady lines through my hair, trembling as I slowly circled the head of his cock with my tongue. The next moan was mine, and he shifted suddenly, grabbing the edge of the bed for balance.

"Oh, God, yes," he moaned. "That's...Seb, that's..." His cock twitched against my tongue, and in turn my own cock ached even more. Much more of this and the hand on his leg would have to be put to use elsewhere because the more this turned him on, the more it turned me on.

Luke had other ideas, though.

"Get up on the bed," he whispered, extending his hand. "On your knees."

He didn't have to tell me twice. I took his hand and he helped me to my feet. Before I could get on the bed, though, he put his arms around me.

"I fucking love what you do with your mouth," he growled and pulled me into a passionate kiss.

I ran my hand down his back and pressed my fingers into the small of his back, gently nudging his hips against mine. Our erections brushed each other, and we both gasped, then moaned into another long, breathless kiss.

"On the bed," he said, panting against my lips. "Now. Please." I nodded, and we separated. While he went for the nightstand drawer, I got on the bed.

The drawer opened. Closed.

Foil tore. A bottle clicked.

And my heart pounded as Luke joined me.

He held my hip with one hand, and I held my breath, waiting for the coolness of the lube and that familiar pressure. When he touched me, I exhaled and willed myself to relax. Whether borne of nerves or excitement, being so tense could make this unpleasant for both of us.

He pressed a little harder, and I pushed back. As soon as the head of his cock slid into me, I didn't just relax, I nearly melted. A low groan escaped my lips as he pushed in slowly, giving me an inch or so before pulling out again. Each time he gave me a little more, withdrew, and did it again. We both knew I didn't need him to ease into me; there was more than enough lube, and I could handle anything he gave me.

He was teasing me. Plain and simple. When I tried to move, rocking my hips back to pull him deeper, he gave a quiet laugh and held my hips in place. *You're at my mercy now*, his grip told my body. *You'll get whatever I see fit to give you.*

Not that it wasn't pleasurable. Every stroke, every longer, deeper stroke, took my breath away. Nerve endings remembered. Anticipation rippled up my spine, knowing what was coming. He was too horny, wanted this too badly, to stay this slow for long.

"Oh my God, Seb," he moaned. He ran his hands up and down my sides and my back, still moving his cock in and out in a slow but progressively less even cadence. "God...you feel..." He blew out a long breath, shuddering as his hands returned to my hips. There they stopped, and I bit my lip as his fingers loosened, tightened, loosened. He was finding his grip. Steadying himself. Grabbing on so he could lose control.

Yes, Luke, yes. Do it. Please, please, please...

That first deep, hard thrust almost knocked my arms out from under me. The second knocked the breath out of me in a single, sharp grunt.

He didn't ask if I was okay. He knew. If I wasn't, I'd let him know, and since I had done no such thing, he didn't back down. He slammed into me again and again, thrusting so deep and hard it hurt, and I suddenly knew the meaning of the phrase "fucking someone blind". My vision blurred with tears, then went completely white. With every stroke, everything was more intense—the pain, the pleasure, the complete and utter delirium—and I couldn't get enough. I was sure I cried out his name, or a string of profanity, or... something. Maybe I just groaned. Whatever I said, he got the message, and he fucked me harder. I screwed my eyes shut, a single hot tear sliding down my cheek.

Just when I thought my vision couldn't get any whiter, the pleasure couldn't get any more painful, and the pain couldn't get any closer to ecstasy, it did. My eyes flew open. A throaty roar escaped my lips. I dug the heels of my hands into the bed and shoved myself back against him, needing him just that much deeper and harder and—

"*Fuck.*" I groaned, shuddered and came like no man but Luke Emerson could ever make me come. My arms very nearly collapsed under me as my orgasm threatened to shake my spine to useless pieces.

And Luke didn't stop. He just didn't stop. His fingers dug into my hips, and he fucked me, kept fucking me, fucked me right up until that moment when too much would have become *way* too much, and in that instant, he took one final thrust and shuddered. He didn't make a sound, didn't even exhale, but the silent intensity of his powerful release reverberated through the air around us.

Finally, he blew out a breath and relaxed against me. For a moment, neither of us moved. We trembled, we panted, but we didn't move.

After a while, his weight shifted, his hand coming down beside mine so I wasn't holding both of us up. His lips touched the base of my neck, and he laughed softly when I shivered.

His hand drifted up my side. "You okay?"

I nodded. Once, slowly, careful not to move suddenly in case my arms decided to give out. "Yeah. Yeah, I'm fine."

He kissed my neck one more time and murmured, "Now *that* is what I call foreplay."

CHAPTER 6

I AWOKE TO THE WARM SOFTNESS OF HIS LIPS BETWEEN my shoulder blades as he worked his way kiss by kiss up to my neck. Every inch of my spine tingled from the center of my back up to where his lips were now, and I shivered as his unshaven jaw brushed my skin.

I reached back, combing my fingers through his hair. It was still damp and cool, so it must not have been long since we'd showered after...Jesus, how many times had we fucked last night?

He nuzzled my neck as his hand drifted up my side, then around to my chest. I closed my eyes when his finger-tips found one of my nipple rings.

"Like that?" His lip brushed my ear.

"Mm-hmm."

He laughed softly. "I figured you would." His released my piercing and his hand drifted down to my stomach. There, he made light circles with his fingertips. At first, the spine-tingling touch just made my abs contract, but then it started getting ticklish. I bit my lip, trying to squirm away from his hand, which meant pushing myself against his body.

"Remember," I said, trying really hard not to laugh, "I know where you're ticklish too."

He grinned against my skin. Then he pulled away slightly. Not backing off, just giving me some room to move, and as soon as I had that room, I rolled onto my back so we could see each other.

I winced as I moved. Every muscle in my body ached. More than a few places would probably be black and blue later. Worth it. Well worth it.

My back landed gently on the bed, and in seconds Luke's lips were against mine. He touched my face, caressing my cheek as his tongue parted my lips. Fatigue still fogged my mind, but my body knew the way. I wrapped my arms around him, letting the heat of his body and the gentleness of his kiss intoxicate me.

When we finally came up for air, he looked down at me and smiled.

"Morning," he murmured, running his fingers through my hair.

I smiled back. "Morning."

"Get some sleep?"

I shrugged. "Enough."

"Good." He grinned and leaned in to kiss me again. "Then you're well-rested for me, aren't you?"

"Or maybe," I said, "you're well-rested for *me*." I gently pushed his shoulder back and, being careful of his freshly tattooed arm, we rolled over together. He lifted his head to kiss me again, but instead of meeting his lips, I went for his neck.

I kissed my way down to his collarbone, then started back up his neck, following that long-memorized map of all those sensitive places: a flick of my tongue below his ear, dragging my lower lip beneath his jaw until he shivered, *almost* sinking my teeth in just above the place his neck met his shoulder.

Don't do this, some quiet little voice whispered in the back of my mind as I continued down Luke's chest.

This is a mistake. I flicked my tongue across his nipple, then circled it, then flicked it again.

Seb, what are you—

"Oh my God..." Luke's voice wasn't much louder, but it was enough to drown those nagging doubts.

Resting on my forearms, I trailed gentle kisses across his abs and onto his side. I made sure my unshaven jaw brushed his skin as my lips did, and laughed when he squirmed. *See, Luke? You're not the only one who remembers all those ticklish places.*

I kissed everywhere around his cock, carefully avoiding it as I teased his lower abs, the groove where thigh met hip, his inner thigh. Anywhere except his cock, grinning to myself as his sharp breaths spoke of arousal and frustration. I inched closer, so close he could probably feel my warm breath where he so desperately wanted to feel my tongue.

This shouldn't be happening, that little voice insisted. *You shouldn't be here.*

I ran the tip of my tongue along the underside of his erection. His back arched off the bed and a whimper escaped his lips.

Seb, don't.

Inch by inch I took his cock into my mouth. Balancing on one arm, I stroked him slowly with my free hand while I teased him with my lips and tongue. Luke moaned and shivered as I found all those sensitive places, all those nerves I'd long ago memorized. The more he fell apart, the more eagerly I sucked him and the more I wanted to fuck him. I was hard as hell now, the ache intensifying with every unsteady breath he drew.

His torso shifted slightly. The sound of the nightstand drawer made my breath catch. Foil tore. I knew exactly what he wanted. I wanted it too, but I wasn't giving this up for the world.

"Seb...oh fuck..." He groaned. "Seb, let me...I want..."

I stroked him faster with both lips and hand, and my cock ached as his groan became another whimper. *Don't worry, Luke, that condom won't go to waste.*

"Fuck, that's amazing," he whispered. "Oh, God..." He was almost sobbing now, his voice shaking the way his body did, the way my hands would have if I'd let go of him just then.

He grabbed my hair, and I was afraid he'd try to stop me, but he didn't. He just held on, fingers twitching against my scalp as his cock twitched against my tongue. I looked up at him. He'd propped himself up on his other arm and looked right back at me, eyes wide and lips parted.

I deep-throated him, and the bed whispered of shifting weight as he sank back down to the pillow.

"Just like that," he groaned. "Fuck, just like..." His hand trembled in my hair. "Don't stop, Seb, don't...oh, *fuck*..." Another groan, a sharp gasp, and hot semen hit my tongue.

When he couldn't take any more, I pushed myself up. As soon as I was within reach, he met my lips in a hungry, breathless kiss, and he wasn't the only one out of breath. We tangled our fingers in each other's hair, both of us shaking, both of us panting, neither of us relenting.

Eventually, he broke the kiss, cradling my neck in trembling hands as he looked up at me.

"Jesus Christ, Seb, your mouth is fucking—"

"Condom." I licked my lips, still struggling to catch my breath. "Give me the condom."

He didn't hesitate. Nor did he give me the condom he already had in his hand. Instead, he reached between us and stroked me gently. Slowly. Jesus, that man could be a tease when he wanted to be.

"Fuck, put it on," I whispered. My eyes rolled back and I struggled just to breathe as his hand teased and tantalized and— "Luke. Put it...put it *on*."

"But I want to tease you," he singsonged in my ear.

"And I need to fuck you."

His fingers tightened briefly, the motion of his hand faltering, and I knew I had him where I wanted him.

"Condom. Now."

No more teasing. He rolled the condom onto my cock. I had to close my eyes and dig my teeth into my bottom lip just to stay in control. It didn't matter how many times we'd done this last night, I needed him again. The lube bottle clicked. I pulled in a breath through gritted teeth as he stroked the lube on, and I was thankful the condom tempered both the coolness of the lube and the heat of his hand. I wanted to make this last, and if he aroused me any more than he already had, it wouldn't.

He released me and whispered, "Should I get on my—"

"No, no, stay just like that." I opened my eyes. "Just... like that." I sat up and ran my hand along his inner thigh, watching his eyes as I used my other hand to guide myself to him.

Seb, don't do it. Don't fucking do it.

I closed my eyes and groaned as I slid my cock into him. The voice in my head quieted. Either it was futile to argue or I just couldn't hear it anymore over my heartbeat and

Luke's long, ragged exhalation. Whatever the case, it shut up.

My back and hips ached with every stroke, but it was bearable as long as I didn't move too fast. That was fine by me; slow and easy was exactly what I wanted right now. There'd been plenty of desperate, violent sex last night.

I leaned down, resting my weight on my forearms and letting my chest brush his each time I moved. I touched my forehead to his. We alternated between kissing lazily and simply breathing each other. He put his hands on my shoulders, pressing just enough to let me know he wanted me to lift myself up. I did, and he moved his hands to my chest. I gasped when he teased my nipple rings with his thumbs. My lips faltered against his, and his curved into a grin.

"Like that?"

I nodded. They were extra sensitive now after a night of being stimulated again and again, and Luke had found just the right amount of pressure to send currents of *oh my fucking God* coursing through every nerve ending that wasn't already sizzling from the ecstasy of being inside him.

I moaned and let my head fall beside his, thrusting a little harder and a little faster than my aching muscles wanted to accommodate. I'd probably pay for it later, but I didn't care. I gritted my teeth and ignored the pain because Luke just felt too damned good. His thumbs on my nipple rings, his breath on my neck, my cock deep inside him. I'd take every ache and twinge my body dished out later in exchange for this.

A violent shudder ran through me. Then another. My eyes rolled back, my nerves turned to liquid electricity, and my entire body trembled as I managed a few last thrusts before—

"Oh...God..." I threw my head back and gasped. With a moan that quickly fell to a whimper, I came.

My body collapsed over his. I had the presence of mind to keep supporting myself on my shaking arms, but he drew me all the way down. I sank against him, closing my eyes and resting my head on his shoulder as he ran his fingers through my hair.

When I was confident my legs might stay under me, I got up just long enough to get rid of the condom. Once that was taken care of, I collapsed on the bed beside him.

We faced each other on our sides.

He grinned. "You're fucking amazing, you know that?"

"So are you." I trailed my fingertips down the side of his face.

He draped his arm over my waist and kissed me lightly. I slid my hand from his face into his hair, and we spent a few lazy minutes just lost in each other's kiss. My hand drifted from his hair to his neck, then to his shoulder, then started down his arm.

The raised edge of his tattoo met my fingertip and I jerked my hand away before he'd even winced.

"Sorry," I murmured.

"It's okay." He grimaced and rolled his shoulder, as if trying to work some stiffness out of that arm.

"How does your arm feel?"

He eyed me, though he couldn't hide the grin. "Both of my arms hurt like hell now, thanks to you."

I laughed. "I mean the one I colored all over."

"Oh, right. It burns, but it's not bad."

"Let me have a look at it."

He lowered his arm so I could see the tattoo. We'd removed the bandage last night, and at some point while we'd caught our breath, I'd put some lotion on it for him. It was still red around the edges now and had just started to scab a little, but it looked fine. Fine, and just as mysterious and—

"It'll probably start to itch in a few days," I said. "Don't scratch it."

"I know, I know." He laughed, putting his arm over me again. "You explained this last night. Twice."

My cheeks burned and I shrugged with one shoulder. "Just trying to make sure you take care of it."

"You would be the expert, wouldn't you?" He trailed his fingers along one of my sleeves.

"I'd better be," I said. "This is how I make my living, remember?"

"True." He propped himself up on one elbow and looked closer at the designs on my arm. "So, are these all part of one big mural type of thing? Or is it just a bunch of small, unrelated tattoos?"

I gestured at my left forearm. "These all represent something about my heritage. See how it's a bunch of smaller images, but they're all connected." With one finger, I traced the intricately detailed roots that connected symbols of my Irish, Scandinavian and Portuguese blood, plus a few nods to some of the Danish, English and Russian that was back there somewhere.

"A family tree," he said, amusement pulling at his mouth. "Creative."

I shrugged. "Seemed like a good idea at the time."

He laughed. "You don't sound so convinced that it's still a good idea."

"Oh, it is." I smiled. "I like it, it just took for-fucking-ever to finish."

"Did you put that one on?"

I shook my head. "No, I had a friend do this sleeve. I

have to really work at it to tattoo with my right hand, so doing it on myself? Not a chance."

"But you did the other?" He nodded toward my right arm.

"Most of it." I held out my arm. "The lower half is still a work-in-progress. The upper half is by the same guy who did the right arm."

He tilted his head and furrowed his brow, inspecting all the intricate details of the myriad abstract and designs that covered from my wrist to my elbow. "These are really cool."

"Thanks."

Our eyes met and we exchanged smiles. He leaned in to kiss me lightly, then grimaced as he started to sit up. Once he was upright, he rubbed his lower back.

"Getting too old for this?" I asked.

He eyed me over his shoulder, and I smirked. He rolled his eyes. "Smartass." With a grunt, he swung his legs over the edge of the bed and stood. "I'm going to go grab a shower." He grinned, and it was that look again. The unspoken invitation.

I smiled. "Give me a few minutes. I don't even know if my legs will hold me up."

"Now who's getting too old for this?"

"Very funny." I rolled my eyes. "My legs are still shaking from fucking you, thank you very much. I'm hardly sore and crippled like you."

He chuckled and leaned down to kiss me. "Still plenty of time for me to leave you sore and crippled."

"At least let me catch my breath."

"Never." He kissed me one more time and stood. "Anyway. I need a shower."

"Careful with the ink." I gestured at his tattoo. "Just rinse it, don't scrub it or anything."

"I know, you mentioned that the last few times we were in the shower."

I laughed. "Just making sure you don't forget."

"I won't, Mom," he said.

After he'd gone into the bathroom, I stared up at the ceiling. It had been way too long since I'd had this kind of sex. All night long, it was breathless and relentless. Without any emotional strings to get tangled, we'd fucked until we were bruised and exhausted. Then we did it one last time for good measure before we grabbed yet another shower and fell asleep.

And this morning. My God. I closed my eyes and couldn't help smiling. Gentle and lazy, just like—

My eyes flew open. Ice slithered through my veins.

Sensual. Tender. Playful.

It had been just like old times.

Just like when we used to make love.

I groaned and rubbed my eyes with the heels of my hands. I knew this would happen. I fucking knew it because it always did. What the fuck was I thinking?

I *never* should have gone to Wilde's last night. I'd have been better off smoking a pack or two of Marlboros and calling it a day. Or spending the night with Kieran. It wasn't possible for me to spend a night with Luke without getting emotionally involved, and I knew it. If we hadn't already crept into that territory, we were perilously close. It was just sex so far, with just a little more intimacy than a couple of strangers might have had in a one night stand, but I knew us. We'd lit the cigarette, even if we hadn't yet taken a drag. I knew where this could go if we let it go even a step further.

The truth I'd known all along throbbed inside my head like a smug, cosmic *I told you so*:

This was a mistake.

CHAPTER 7

As I gathered my clothes, I kept one ear tuned to the sound of running water in the next room. My hands shook as I dressed as quickly as I could, certain the shower would cut off at any moment. The fact that he'd invited me to join him meant I had time on my side—he'd wait at least a few minutes before he figured out I wasn't coming—but I rushed nonetheless.

I finished tying my shoes and checked to make sure I had my wallet and keys. Still sitting on the bed, I tapped my fingers on the nightstand.

Crap. Now what? I chewed my thumbnail and stared at the bathroom door. Did I just leave? Disappear on him like a damned coward?

Walk away. Just walk away before it gets more complicated than it already is.

I rubbed my forehead and sighed. It wasn't that complicated. In my head it was, but in reality? So what if we'd had sex? So what if we'd even made love? We weren't *in* love. We weren't back together. I could still walk away from this unscathed and with some semblance of dignity. I could still get through his next appointment without losing a shred of professionalism.

Couldn't I?

I closed my eyes and blew out a breath. I was overreacting. Plain and simple. I had no reason to think this was going to get that out of hand after one night.

No reason except that it had happened so many times before. No reason except this was unnervingly like far too many mornings after.

The shower stopped. So did my heart. While I waited for him to come out, I breathed slowly, evenly, willing myself not to panic. Not to freak out. I'd just wait until he came out here, then calmly bow out, get out, and leave before this went too far.

The bathroom door opened.

I opened my eyes.

My heart started beating again. Fast. Too fast.

His dark hair was still wet, spiky, tousled from the towel that was now around his waist. A few stray drops on his chest and shoulders caught the light. He stopped in his tracks, confusion furrowing his brow as he looked me up and down, probably wondering why the hell I was dressed, and as I looked at him now, I wondered the same thing.

I swallowed hard. I should have left before he'd turned off the water, because this had already gone too far.

He cocked his head. "Seb, what are—"

"I have to go," I said quickly.

"What? Why?"

I gritted my teeth and got to my feet. "This was a bad idea."

"You didn't seem to think it was a bad idea last night," he snapped. "Or this morning."

I glared at him. "Look, I try not to make a habit of sleeping with my clients."

"Clients?" He narrowed his eyes. "So that's what I am? Just a client you decided to fuck?"

I shrugged. "Okay, I don't make a habit of fucking serial cheaters from my past."

Anger flashed in his eyes, and he opened his mouth to speak, but his expression quickly shifted to a less hostile one. A mid-breath change of tactics. He stepped toward me and laid a gentle hand on my arm. "Don't go. Please. Can we at least talk about this?"

I swallowed hard. Just looking at him hurt. We'd been here before. The reunion. The fucking. The lovemaking. The talking. Ultimately, we'd get back together. Then he'd hurt me again, and in time, we'd play this little game once more.

"Seb, please," he whispered. "Can we talk about this?"

"I'd rather not." The words were colder than I intended, but I made no apologies for that.

"There are still things I need to say. Please, we—"

"There's nothing left to talk about." I avoided his eyes and shrugged away from his touch. "This was supposed to be about a tattoo. A business transaction." I exhaled. "I never should have come here."

Without looking at him, I took a step back. Though I was still less than an arm's length away, he didn't reach for me this time.

"Seb..."

Step. "I'm sorry, Luke." Step. "I shouldn't—" Another step, and with the increasing distance between us came the spine to speak again. "I shouldn't be here." With that, I turned to go, and I kept going before I could give myself a chance to reconsider. My jacket was still on the floor where it had fallen last night. I picked it up and kept right on going.

Mercifully, he didn't call after me. When the door closed behind me, clicking shut after I'd already descended the front steps, it didn't open again. Thank God he wasn't as persistent as he'd been in his younger days, because I didn't know how many times I could walk away from him.

The cunning bastard knew full well how much I loved sex with him. A night like that, a morning like this, and few men in their right mind would be difficult to persuade to stick around for more. Then again, few men in their right mind would have been stupid enough to show up at Wilde's last night, regardless of the sex that awaited.

What the fuck was I thinking?

Thinking with my dick, of course. I muttered a few curses into the crisp morning air. I'd fallen for this one too many times. Not again. I'd take last night for the physically satisfying, scorching hot sex that it was, and move on without any emotional bullshit.

Right. And convincing myself of that *before* the clothes had come off had worked so well. Live and learn. It was over. Again. Time to move on. Again. At least this time it ended before it had a chance to really start.

I caught a bus a few blocks from Luke's apartment and dropped my sore, aching carcass into one of the stained, tattered seats. Resting my elbow below the window, I closed my eyes and let my forehead fall into my hand.

One night. One goddamned night. What the hell was I thinking when I thought I could spend a single night with him without getting more involved than just sex? I could do one-night stands and casual sex, but not with him, not even after all this time.

Just one night with him, and we'd opened a Pandora's

box of memories. I'd held on to all of the bad things—the cheating, the lying, the fighting—for dear life over the past four years, and I'd shoved almost everything else into the back of my mind. I remembered the sex and all the other things I could convince myself were superficial and meaningless. I'd hidden everything that wasn't so superficial and meaningless behind everything that still hurt.

Little by little, though, it all came back.

My mind drifted back to a night we'd spent out on the balcony of my old apartment. Just the two of us, sitting in a couple of mismatched plastic patio chairs with a wobbly plastic table and an ashtray between us, staring up at the night sky. We hadn't yet moved in together, so we must have been nineteen or so. A year into college, the first of four years of endless days spent working our asses off at two or three different jobs between fucking, drinking and cutting classes.

Somehow, amidst all the self-induced chaos, we always found time for nights like this. Just Luke, me and a pack of Marlboros that would go up in smoke before morning.

And we talked. About anything, everything and nothing at all, we talked.

"So, have you told your parents yet?" he'd asked on that particular night.

I'd snorted as I reached for the shared pack of cigarettes. "Fuck no. Are you crazy?"

"You're going to have to tell them eventually, you know."

I groaned. "I really don't want to think about that."

Luke laughed. "Come on, they probably won't be as upset about it as you think. And if they are, hell, fuck 'em."

I looked at him, eyebrows up. "Easy for you to say."

He shrugged. "What's the big deal, though? It's not exactly traditional, but there's nothing *wrong* with it."

"Maybe not as long as someone *else's* kid is doing it." I slid a smoke free, then held the pack out to him, but he shook his head. I went on. "They'll have fucking heart failure if they find out."

"Why? There are worse things you could be doing."

"Yeah, maybe." I raised the cigarette, but stopped just shy of my lips. "Seriously, my parents will kill me if I tell them I'm doing this as a hobby, let alone making a career out of it."

Another shrug. "So what? It's your life, not theirs."

"Yeah, I know, but..." I shook my head, then focused on lighting my cigarette.

"Just think about it, Seb. Your folks are cool. Would they really want you doing something that made you miserable?"

"At this point, I think they'd just rather I did anything that meant they didn't have to support my ass." I took a drag off the freshly lit cigarette.

"And doing this would mean you're making a living, so they wouldn't have to support you." He plucked the cigarette from my hand and kept his eyes locked on mine while he brought it up to his lips to take a drag. Then he blew out a thin stream of smoke and went on. "Besides, you can make a pretty damned good living as a tattoo artist." He set the cigarette between my fingers again. I didn't mind. They always seemed to taste better after he'd had a drag anyway.

"It takes a while to get to that point, though."

He shrugged. "But you're good at it. You know I'm not just saying that. Your work is phenomenal."

"Thanks." I smiled, then set the cigarette between my lips. It *did* taste better.

He shot me a mischievous grin. "I could always tell them next time we're there for dinner."

I laughed, releasing a wisp of gray smoke into the night. "Don't you fucking dare."

"Then you talk to them."

"I will."

"When?"

"Eventually."

He sighed dramatically. "Sebastian, has anyone ever told you you're a complete chickenshit when it comes to your parents?"

I chuckled and took one last drag. "Guilty as charged." I snuffed out the cigarette and rested my hand on the armrest.

Luke reached past the wobbly table with the ashtray on it and slipped his hand into mine. When he spoke, the humor was gone from his voice. "Listen, even if they don't support you, they'll get over it. It's your life, not theirs, so it's not their decision to make." He squeezed my hand and smiled at me under the dim glow of the dying porch light. "And you know you'll always have my support."

I returned the smile. "I know."

I opened my eyes to the harsh sunlight of the present day, resisting the urge to curse aloud as the memory drifted back into the distant past.

More than the cheating, the lying and the fighting, I hated him for those nights.

Muttering a few choice obscenities under my breath, I pulled the stop request chain, and a moment later, the bus stopped in front of the convenience store several blocks from my apartment. The convenience store which, of course, had nothing to do with why I'd asked the driver to let me off here. Not in the least.

Especially when I knew full well there was another stop less than fifty yards from my front door.

River. Egypt.

I went into the convenience store and didn't bother trying to fool myself into believing I wanted a soda or a magazine. I went right up to the counter.

"A pack of Marlboros and a lighter, please." Guilt and resignation pressed my shoulders down.

The clerk didn't ask for identification. He'd sold me both cigarettes and beer countless times in the past. That, and I'd tattooed seven Chinese characters down the middle of his back. It was safe to say he knew me well enough to know I was over eighteen.

"I thought you'd quit." He eyed me as he scanned the pack.

I shifted my weight. "Tried to."

"Again?"

I forced a smile, forcing myself not to grab him by the collar and tell him to quit fucking around and give me the damned cigarettes. I drummed my fingers on the counter. *God, I really do need a smoke, don't I?*

After I'd paid, the clerk handed me my debit card and the coveted pack of Marlboros. Then I hurried outside and headed home. On the way up the sidewalk, I stared at the pack in my hand. My mouth watered and my hands shook. I'd already paid for them and all but resigned myself to having one. Might as well.

I tamped the pack against the inside of my wrist. Just that routine, the first of several steps between now and that first drag, soothed my jumpy nerves.

Before I could get the cellophane off the pack, though, a

flicker of willpower worked itself to the surface from somewhere deep inside and ignited enough rational thought to get my attention. I already felt like shit over last night and this morning. I'd given in to temptation and gotten tangled up with my ex. Did I really want to add a relapsed smoking habit to the guilty, self-loathing mix?

With a frustrated sigh, I shoved the unopened pack into my back pocket. Right where I'd always kept them, but better to have the whole pack there than one in my mouth.

I kept walking. Every step worked out some of the stiffness and soreness from last night, and for that I was thankful. The less I felt it, the less real it was.

When I got home, I considered just going across the street to the shop and getting right to work, but I keyed myself into my apartment anyway. The sooner I got to work, the sooner I could focus on getting back to life before Luke, but first, one thing I definitely needed was a shower. I tossed the cigarettes on the coffee table, threw my jacket over the back of a chair, and went in to take a shower.

As I undressed, I glanced in the mirror and did a double take. Just in front of my hipbone was a faint bruise. At first I thought it was just a shadow, but when I turned to get a better look, it was still there. I tried to place it, racking my brain to remember just how I'd gotten it. I put my hand on my hip and sure enough, my fingers fit right over it. It was tender, though not terribly painful, and I wasn't at all surprised to see a similar bruise on my other hip.

...he held my hips and slammed into me. "Harder, fuck me harder..."

I shook my head and turned away to turn on the water, pretending the memory and the marks he'd left hadn't sent pleasant chills through me. Chills that the water would warm, thank God, so I stepped into the shower and—

God damn you, Luke.

Even the hot water on my skin reminded me of him. Of last night. Of everything we'd done from the bedroom to the shower and back again. Even if this morning was too intimate, last night was undeniably hot. Just thinking of him made me hard, as if he were standing right here with that grin on his face. The heat on my skin had nothing on the heat beneath it, the fire in my veins that Luke had always been able to ignite with a touch, a look, even a memory.

After all of that, I shouldn't have had anything left, but damn it, I did.

I wrapped my fingers around my cock and gave in to the images in my mind. Stroking in time with the thrusts in my memory, I went back to sometime after midnight when I'd driven myself deep inside him and he'd begged me not to stop, never to stop, don't fucking stop. Just before sunrise, when we were so tired we could barely move, and still he bent me over the bed and fucked me. When he'd left those bruises on my hips. His cock inside me. My knees trembling. Seeing stars, seeing white. His breathless, growling voice beside my ear right when I let go. The throaty groan when he did.

I moaned into the whisper of falling water and came. It was one of the most anticlimactic orgasms I'd ever had. Enough to soothe the ache and take the edge off, but it barely even knocked me off balance. It certainly didn't make me feel any better.

I rested my forehead against the cool, wet tile. He just had to come back into my life, didn't he? Because what I'd needed right now, more than anything in the world, was a reminder of what I didn't have anymore. A taste of something I'd never come close to replacing.

We certainly weren't virgins when we met, but we

might as well have been for as nervous as we both were the first time we slept together. Neither of us could remember how to work buttons or belt buckles. I accidentally bumped his cheekbone with my elbow in the midst of taking my shirt off. He moved in a little too enthusiastically for a kiss and caught my lip against the edge of my tooth. The condom wrapper was apparently modeled after Fort Knox, because it took both of us to get the damned thing open.

It should have been awkward and embarrassing, tripping over our proverbial feet like that, but it wasn't. We laughed. In bed, having sex for the first clumsy time together, we *laughed*.

That was when I knew, an illusion though it may have been, we were in for the long haul. We were more than a fling and a fuck. We could be so unashamedly imperfect—in bed, in conversation, in every way—so we were perfect for each other.

Before Luke, sex had always been such an urgent, serious thing. Not with him, though. Right from the start, we'd laughed. At first, nervousness. With time, as we became accustomed to each other, playfulness. Sometimes we got carried away, like the time he made me laugh—and hell if I could remember what it was about—while I was going down on him. It caught me so off guard, I'd nearly choked, which in turn made him laugh. We both lost it, feeding off each other until we were both in total hysterics. Of course that meant that once we'd caught our breath, we had to start all over with the foreplay, but neither of us minded.

It wasn't always like that. Sometimes we were just too desperate, too overwhelmed with need for each other, and it could be anything from quietly intense to furniture-breaking violent. Sometimes it was physical, sometimes it was emotional, sometimes it was both. Quickies. All nighters. We had gentle sex, angry sex, makeup sex, drunk sex.

And it wasn't enough for him.

My heart sank a little further. Tears stung my eyes. It may have been years ago, but it still hurt like hell knowing that for all he'd satisfied me, I was never enough to keep him from seeking more elsewhere.

So why did you keep going back, Sebastian? Why?

I knew why. I always let him come back because I'd loved him. Each time I'd hoped he'd really changed, and surprise, surprise, he hadn't.

Though I tried to think of anything but, this morning crept into my consciousness again. The way we'd held each other. The playful intimacy. The gentle kissing and touching.

I released a long breath as my heart sank even deeper.

The worst part was the realization that no matter how much I'd wished all kinds of things on him over the years, no matter how many hexes and curses I'd have put on him had I known how, one thing was painfully clear now: I still loved him.

Fuck my life, I still loved him. Nothing in the world hurt like realizing I could still be in love with someone after everything he'd done to me.

But damn it, I was.

CHAPTER 8

FOR THE NEXT TWO WEEKS, EVERY MOMENT OF MY LIFE was calibrated to seven o'clock on Friday night. Every tattoo was one step closer to A.J.'s angel. Every inch of skin I covered in ink was another piece of a map leading me straight toward that appointment. That tattoo. That man.

I had no idea if he'd even show up. He didn't have to. The tattoo was outlined. All that was left was the fine detail work and shading. He could have left it as is, or let any tattooist on the planet finish it. Normally, I bristled at the idea of another artist touching my work, but this time, I hoped he'd have someone else do it. Artwork be damned, I didn't know if I could look at him again, let alone sit for another hour and a half with my hands on him.

I didn't have much choice, though, because at six forty-five on Friday night, Luke walked into my shop.

We made eye contact over the counter, but it didn't last more than a few seconds. Gone was the cocky smugness he'd brought in here the first day.

I looked up from a tattoo-in-progress and acknowledged

him with the same *I'll be right with you* nod I gave any customer when I was busy with someone else.

Luke didn't say a word. He took a seat on the opposite side of the counter while I continued with my client. The shop was hardly quiet. Two needles buzzed. A hard rock album played in the background. Jason was halfway through the second of three college girls who'd come in to get tiny tats on their ankles, and they giggled and squealed while he worked. On any other night, I'd have laughed to myself and shaken my head at their obvious attempts to flirt with him, but I wasn't in the mood for it tonight. I just focused on the lines and dots on my client's shoulder. I pretended my nerves weren't twisting and coiling like the elaborate snake in front of me, the green and red serpent slithering in the mouth and out the eye socket of a skull.

Not on Luke. Not in the least.

Little by little, tattoos were finished and the shop's population diminished. Every jingle of the bells marked the gradual reduction of several to two. The college girls paid and left. I bandaged my own client's tattoo, settled up the bill, and scheduled an appointment to work on his half-sleeve. Then he, too, was gone.

Jason was still there, though, so neither Luke nor I spoke as I set up for his tattoo. Under normal circumstances, I'd have had everything mostly set up before he ever walked through the door. Even when he showed up fifteen minutes early, I'd have been nearly ready to start.

But I wasn't ready for him. I'd been busy with this walk-in and running late because of it. Even if I hadn't been with a client, I doubt I'd have been ready, because I'd convinced myself Luke wasn't coming in. I sighed and shook my head. I was starting to get really good at making myself believe things.

About the time I had everything ready to go for Luke's tattoo, Jason came out of the back office. He picked up his jacket and helmet. "I'm out of here unless you need me for anything else." His eyes darted toward Luke, then back to me, and his eyebrows rose.

"Nope, I'm good." I gestured toward the door. "See you tomorrow."

He touched his forehead in a fake salute. "Adios."

The bells rang, and I was alone with Luke. Alone, set up, with nowhere to go but here.

"You ready for this?" I asked, trying and failing to inject some humor into my voice.

"Yeah, I think so." When I glanced at him, his Adam's apple bobbed. I wondered if he was more nervous about facing me or the tattoo needle. I nodded toward the chair.

He came around the counter but hesitated to take a seat. "Listen, you don't have to do this."

"I started it." I gestured at the chair again. "I need to finish it."

"But if it's—"

"You said you wanted my work."

He swallowed. "Yeah, of course. That's why I came to you. But I don't—"

"Luke, please," I said, almost whispering. "Just sit so we can both be done with this."

He hesitated again, then sat. Thankfully, he'd worn a T-shirt this time, so all I had to do was roll the sleeve up and clip it into place. The silence lingered as I adjusted his sleeve, took my own seat and prepped his skin. When the buzzing needle filled that silence, Luke closed his eyes and breathed slowly and deeply. I doubted that would last, if his previous appointment was any indication.

I put the needle to his skin, and sure enough, the deep

breathing turned into held breaths. Professionalism trumped awkwardness. I didn't need a passed-out client on my hands, and talking meant breathing. As long as we didn't talk about *us*, we'd be okay.

"So, any idea what you'll be doing once you're finished with your degree?"

Luke exhaled through his nose but didn't open his eyes. "Making more money, I hope."

"That's kind of the idea, isn't it?" I said, chuckling.

"In theory." He looked at me, those ice blue eyes sending a pleasant shudder down my spine. "But I have to wonder if all the tuition and shit doesn't offset any money I might— ow, *Jesus*."

"Oh, come on, it doesn't hurt that bad."

"Pfft." He shot me a playful glare. "Says the man who doesn't have a needle in his skin."

I laughed. "And I'm dangerously close to having more skin that's inked than not, so I think I know what it feels like. Just breathe, you'll be fine." I continued shading the stripes on the folded American flag in the angel's arms. As soon as the needle touched his skin, Luke took a long breath and held it, but after a moment, released it.

He must have caught on to the notion that talking could distract him from the pain, because he didn't let the silence linger this time. "So, how long ago did you quit smoking?"

My eyes flicked up as I dipped the needle in red ink. "How did you know I'd quit?" *A cigarette. God. I could go for one right now. Just one. Just—* Stop it, Seb. I touched needle to flesh again.

Luke grimaced. "I couldn't—" He paused. "I couldn't taste it."

Our eyes met. I swallowed hard.

He cleared his throat. "That, and in twelve hours or so, I never once saw you light up."

I focused on the tattoo and tried to keep us on the subject of my broken habit of smoking instead of us. "I quit about four months ago."

"Good, that's great."

"What about you?" I glanced up from adding a little color to the angel's cheeks. "I take it you gave it up too?"

He nodded. "Two years ago."

"Man, I hope I stick with it that long." I rinsed the needle and changed colors, this time going for yellow to highlight the halo and the angel's hair. "This is my seventh attempt."

"Hey, giving that shit up is hard. Took me three tries."

"This had damn well better be my last," I muttered.

"Good luck with it. I almost relapsed myself when—" He stopped abruptly. I looked up just in time to see him glance down at the tattoo before he returned his gaze to the safety of the ceiling. "Anyway," he said, barely whispering, "it's not an easy thing to do."

"No, definitely not," I said quietly.

The silence went for a few minutes, unfilled except by the buzzing needle and his occasional catch of breath. Once again, it was Luke who spoke first.

"So, are you, um, are you seeing anyone these days?"

My eyes flicked up and met his. "If I was, the other night wouldn't have happened."

He had the good graces to darken a little in the cheeks as he looked up at the ceiling. "Right. I guess it wouldn't have. Sorry, that wasn't what I was implying."

"Don't worry about it." I considered asking him the same thing, but with the unanswered questions about A.J., thought it best to leave it be.

Luke coughed into his other hand. "Listen, about the other night…"

It was my turn to hold my breath. I lifted the needle of his arm and took my foot off the pedal. The buzzing died, and my chair creaked as I sat back.

He turned to look at me. "I didn't think, when I came in here that night, that anything would happen. I really didn't."

I cocked my head. "Then—"

"I'm serious, Seb." He dropped his gaze, wetting his lips before meeting my eyes again. "I only came in here for a tattoo. And…to talk."

"We didn't do a hell of a lot of talking that night." I opened and closed my gloved right hand, trying to resist the urge to reach for the non-existent pack of smokes in my back pocket. "Here or…there."

"I know," he whispered. "But it, well, it happened. There's not much I can do to change that."

I shrugged with one shoulder. "True. I suppose the past can't be changed." The slight lift of his eyebrow told me the faint note of bitterness in my voice had found its mark. Beyond that, though, he didn't acknowledge it.

"You left so quickly that morning," he said, "I didn't get a chance to talk to you."

I tapped my fingers on the workstation beside the cups of ink. "Well, we have nothing but time now."

"I guess I'd hoped we could talk a bit about, you know, the past," he said. "Maybe put a few things to rest."

I dipped the needle and leaned in to work on his arm again. The sooner I finished this damned thing, the better. As I worked, I said, "So you wanted to bury the hatchet over a tattoo?"

"It crossed my mind, yes."

I chewed my lip as I concentrated on the angel's gleaming halo. So many questions still lingered. So much I needed to know and was afraid to ask.

I didn't realize how much time had passed since either of us had spoken until he added, "If you're willing to, anyway."

Wiping some excess ink from his skin, I looked up. "It's been a long time. I guess I don't see any need *not* to bury it." *Except as long as I tell myself I hate you, I can pretend I don't love you.* My throat tightened around the unspoken words, and I quickly shifted my attention back to the halo.

"We did have a lot of good times back then," he said quietly.

"I know." *And those hurt more than you can imagine.*

"And I know I—"

"Luke." I took the needle from his skin and looked up again. "I'm willing to let it go and move on. But let's not drag it all back to the surface."

He held my gaze for a moment, then nodded. "Okay. We don't have to." The words were tentative. He probably knew as well as I did that this was far from settled. We'd put it on the table, acknowledged it, but it wasn't over.

It was probably best discussed under other circumstances, though.

"Do you remember the look on my sister's face when she found out we were dating?" he asked with a cautious laugh.

I couldn't help chuckling. "Oh God, I remember that. Poor girl." This I could deal with for now. Talking about our past but not talking about our past. "How did she not know, anyway? I mean, that was after what, almost a year?"

He shook his head. "I have no idea. I didn't make that big of a deal about being gay, but I hardly hid it." He grinned at me. "Actually, I don't think she was shocked about *me* being gay."

I raised an eyebrow. "What do you mean?"

"I think she was a little disappointed to find out you played for the other team."

"What?" I rolled my eyes and reached for the ink again. "Get out of here."

"I'm serious," he said. "I swear to God, she had an insane crush on you."

"And you never told me this, why?"

He snorted. "What the fuck would you have done about it?"

I shrugged. "Oh, I don't know, I was young and—"

"My sister, Sebastian," he growled. "You wouldn't have laid a hand on her."

"Not even if I was a bit curious about women?"

"She's not 'women', she's my sister."

"Which means she has—"

"Oh God," he groaned. "Don't *even* go there." He laughed and shook his head. "So, were you curious about women?"

"Nah, I was just fucking with you." I rinsed the needle and dipped it again. "Did your folks ever get their head around the fact that you're gay?"

He sighed. "My mom has come a long way. She's still not happy about it, but she's more or less gotten over it. As for Dad, well, he's getting there. Slowly."

"I guess that's a good thing," I said quietly. Luke's parents had flipped their lids when he came out. It was just as well he'd already moved in with me at that point, because they'd have thrown him out if he still lived at home. Watching him go through that had made me count my blessings that my parents had accepted me from day one.

Granted they had my history as an epic fuck-up to put things in perspective. They may not have hoped for a gay son, but they were probably just glad to be sitting at the kitchen table listening to me say "Mom, Dad, I'm gay" rather than finding more drug paraphernalia in my bedroom or picking me up at the police station again.

Luke flinched as the needle crept into that sensitive territory around the back of his arm.

"Sorry," I said. "This part won't take long."

"Thank God for that," he muttered. "So. Anyway. My parents are coming around slowly. I never thought they would."

"I wondered about that myself." I paused, carefully shading the narrow feathers of the angel's wing tips. "Glad to hear it, though."

"Funny what time can do to people, I guess."

I looked up and wasn't at all surprised he was looking right back at me. I chewed the inside of my cheek. "Yeah. I guess it is."

Time changed people, that much was clear. But how much? Enough?

It didn't matter. We'd gone down this road too many times before, and we just couldn't do it again. I couldn't do it again.

Not even if I wanted to.

Which I didn't.

Neither of us spoke as I finished shading the last of the tattoo. Fortunately, I was almost done, so the awkward silence didn't last long. Before I knew it, we were done.

With the tattoo bandaged and money settled up, we looked at each other.

Panic and relief tingled at my nerve endings, opposite reactions converging at the base of my spine.

It was over. The tattoo was done. Once he walked out that door, our paths had no reason to ever cross again. Unless, of course, he wanted me to add the years of A.J.'s birth and death. And maybe he would. Maybe he kept those as an ace up his sleeve. A reason for us to breathe the same air at some undetermined tomorrow. A reason for me to touch him.

At least for now, he kept that card close to his chest.

"I guess," he said, avoiding my eyes, "this is it. I, um..." He gestured at his arm. "Thanks. It looks great."

"It'll look better in a week or so." I cleared my throat. "Just, you know, take care of it."

He nodded. "I will." He extended a hand. "Thanks again."

I hesitated, then extended my own hand, pretending the platonic handshake didn't light fuses all up and down the length of my spine. I cleared my throat. "No problem."

He released my hand and turned to go, but made it only a couple of steps before he stopped. He faced me again. Rubbing the back of his neck with one hand, he looked at the floor as he whispered, "Listen, I..."

I watched him. Waited. My heart thundered faster and faster with each silent second that ticked by. Faster still when our eyes met.

"Fuck," he whispered, dropping his gaze again. "I can't...all I can..." He made a frustrated gesture. Then he looked me in the eye and blurted out, "There's a lot I want to say right now, but all I can think is how badly I really, really want to kiss you."

No. No. We can't do this. Say no, say no.

I didn't realize I'd moistened my lips until his eyes flicked down, and by then it was too late to stop myself.

He moved closer to me, and only the shaking in my

knees prevented me from taking a step back. We couldn't, we shouldn't, but my mouth watered nonetheless. I hated myself for wanting this, but want it I did.

Chewing my lower lip, I made the next move, inching closer to him. For a long moment, we were still, just looking at each other. Holding my breath, I dropped my gaze and watched my own hand reach across the divide toward his waist, my heart thundering in my ears as my fingers found his shirt, then the subtle warmth of proximity, and finally the heat of his body. I let my hand rest there, still staring in disbelief at this contact that I had created. We'd gone there. I'd gone there.

Seb, don't.

He touched my face and, with the faintest hint of pressure, raised my chin so I looked him in the eye. When he put his other hand on my waist, I almost collapsed under the weight of his featherlight touch. I watched him run the tip of his tongue along the inside of his lower lip and my mouth watered as I imagined him doing the same to my lip, just as he'd done a million times before.

"Are you sure about this?" he whispered.

"No." My hand moved to his back, pulling him closer.

"Neither am I." The words vibrated against my skin.

I put my free hand on his face, the hiss of my fingertips across stubble just barely audible over the sound of our slow, uneven breaths.

We were so close, breathing each other, his mouth not quite touching mine, but he made no move to close the distance that remained. My hand went from his face to the back of his neck, but still the gap remained between us, and he made no move to close it.

He was waiting for me.

Letting me cross this line.

He was waiting on the other side, but I had to take this step.

Seb. Don't.

Ignoring that little voice, I slid my hand from his neck into his hair and drew him into a kiss. My lips touched his, and he pulled me closer, running the pad of his thumb across my cheekbone. We moved in slow motion. My senses savored every taste and breath of him, my fingertips exploring the rough texture of his jaw as my tongue explored the soft warmth of his mouth.

This wasn't the desperation with which we'd kissed at Wilde's. It wasn't the kind of passionate, violent kiss that gave us an excuse to get lost and forget to think. Though he overwhelmed my senses, everything happened slowly enough to let rational thought catch up. To remember what happened last time we gave in like this.

I pulled back slightly, and his lips released mine.

I sighed. "What are we doing?"

"Kissing, I think."

Our eyes met, and we both laughed nervously.

Then I whispered, "I'm serious. What are...what is this?"

He shook his head slowly. "I don't know. I really don't."

We were quiet for a long moment. I didn't know whether to take the wise, sensible route and talk this over, or just pull him to me and kiss him again. I knew which way I wanted to go, but not which way I should.

Forcing myself not to look at his eyes or his lips, I pulled away. I reached back to rub the back of my neck, just to give my hand something to do that wasn't touching him.

"What was it you wanted to say?" I nodded toward the empty chair and workstation where our aborted conversation had occurred. "Earlier, I mean."

Luke released a ragged breath. He rested one hip against the counter, and a prickly chill of uncertainty descended between my shoulder blades as I waited for him to speak.

"I, um." He swallowed hard. "I wanted to apologize."

"For?"

"Everything." He hesitated. "Everything that happened. You know, back then. All the things I did. That's why I came. I mean, besides the tattoo, that's what I—"

"You came to apologize?" Sudden anger flared in my chest, catching even me off guard. "Was that before or after I put out?"

"Seb, I—"

"Did you figure I'd be more pliable once we'd fucked a few times?" I folded my arms across my chest and took another step back from him. "Like I always was back then?"

He shook his head and showed his palms. "No, no, it wasn't like that at all. When I came here the other night, I had no intention of sleeping with you."

"Is that right?" I shifted my weight. "Then why the hell—"

"You came to Wilde's." His eyes narrowed. "Don't tell me you didn't want that to happen the other night. If you didn't, you wouldn't have come to the club."

"And I'm sure you'd have been heartbroken, wouldn't you?" I growled. "God knows I probably wasn't the only man in that room you probably could have charmed into bed."

"Seb, Jesus, we—"

"Did you think sex was going to magically fix everything?"

"No, of course not." He paused, his eyes darting away from mine. "Sex broke it. It's sure as hell not going to fix it."

"Then why the fuck was I in your bed the other night?"

He glared at me. "Because I couldn't resist you, and I didn't want to resist you any more than *you* wanted to resist *me*, or you wouldn't have been at Wilde's."

I balked. I couldn't argue with him, and I hated him for all of this as much as I hated myself for it.

"Obviously some things haven't changed, then," I growled. "You and temptation have been good buddies for a long time, haven't you?"

"I don't think you understand, Seb," he said softly. "I wasn't horny for any man who was willing. It was you and no one else. If you hadn't shown up, I'd have gone home alone."

A cough of sarcastic laughter burst out of me. "That'll be the day."

"Christ, Sebastian, are you unfamiliar with the concept of forgiveness? Even after all this time? People do change, you know."

"Yes, I know," I said as calmly as I could. "And I might be able to forgive, but that doesn't mean I can forget."

"It was four years ago. Do you think I'd come crawling back after all this time if I didn't—"

"Do you think I'd still be this guarded around you after all this time if it didn't hurt that badly?"

Luke's shoulders dropped. "I'm sorry, Seb. I can't change the past, but I *am* sorry about it. In the last four years, I haven't gone a day without thinking of you and what I did to you, and if there was a way to prove to you that I wouldn't dream of doing it again, then I would."

I looked away, refusing to let him see the tears that stung my eyes. God, I wanted to believe him, and that only made me angrier, though I wasn't sure if that anger was directed more at myself than at him. When I was sure I'd blinked away the evidence that this was killing me, I looked at him again. Through gritted teeth, I whispered unsteadily, "How many times did I hear that back then?"

He put his hands up and shook his head. "Fine. I'm not going to grovel any more than I already have. I'm sorry. That's all I can say." Then his eyes narrowed. "But if you can look me in the eye and tell me you didn't feel a damned thing the other night, then you're a better liar now than I ever was."

I forced myself not to break eye contact. "It doesn't matter what I felt then. It was one night, and it was just sex." I paused, taking a deep breath and willing my voice not to crack. "You of all people should have no difficulty with that, or was there more to it back then too? With all the other guys?"

"No," he whispered. "It was just sex with them."

"And the other night," I said, cursing the lump that tried to rise in my throat, "it was just sex with me."

He flinched, staring at the floor between us for a moment. When our eyes met again, he said, "Even if it was, it doesn't change the fact that I regret everything I did to you back then, and—"

"You've changed, you're a different person, things would be different," I said, the sarcasm masking the unsteadiness in my voice. "I've heard it all before."

He pinched the bridge of his nose, then threw his hands up. "I don't know what else to say, then." The frustration in both voice and posture pissed me off more than anything, as if I was simply being stubborn and had no reason to dig my heels in like this.

"What am I supposed to think, Luke?" I snarled. "You cheated on me. You lied to me. You played me for a fucking idiot. Then you walked away and left me to pick up the pieces. Now you come strolling back into my life and what am I supposed to do? Volunteer to be your goddamned doormat again? At least until I was done writing some other guy's name on—"

My teeth snapped shut. I hadn't intended to play that card, and the words were out before I could stop them.

Luke's eyes widened and his lips parted.

I released a breath. "Luke, I didn't mean—"

"You know *nothing* about A.J.," he growled.

"I know, I'm sorry, I didn't—"

"Yeah, I'll just bet you are." He turned to go.

"Luke, wait. Please, I—"

The door flew open in a sharp chorus of angry bells, then banged shut with more of the same, and I was alone.

CHAPTER 9

I DIDN'T SLEEP THAT NIGHT. THE NEXT DAY, I DODGED questions from Jason about Luke while I worked on tattoos. I offered just enough conversation to keep people from passing out.

By eight or so, the shop was deserted. Jason had gone for the night, and my last appointment was inked, bandaged and out the door. The bells above the door had long fallen quiet. Only the buzzing of my needle kept the eerie silence at bay.

I dipped the needle in red ink and furrowed my brow as I focused on shading the abstract pattern on the edge of my right sleeve. Once I was done with this area, which was about three square inches along the side of my wrist, the lower half of the sleeve would be done. The upper half had to wait until the end of the month when I had an appointment with another artist friend. I could ink my own skin without much difficulty, but the upper arm was a little difficult for me to see well enough to do it right.

This part, however, would be my work, and I was glad to do it right now. Coping with pain as I inflicted it on myself made for the perfect mindset: I couldn't think of anything but lines and pain.

Usually, anyway.

If I wasn't thinking about the other night, when we'd parted ways in this very place, then I was stuck in our past. We had the kind of history that made it easy to hate him and even easier to fall in love with him again. I knew what this could be. How good it could be, how badly it could end. I just didn't know if the good was worth the risk of the bad.

That may or may not have been an option anyway. Luke hadn't suggested getting back together. He'd asked for forgiveness, nothing more. The sex had happened, yes, but he hadn't prefaced it with a plea for another chance. Maybe his pursuit of forgiveness was genuine this time. At least until I'd opened my mouth, that is.

He'd lost someone. Someone dear enough to warrant a tribute in blood and ink. I cringed. Someone whose death and tattoo I'd thrown in his face.

I closed my eyes and let out a breath. I still couldn't believe I'd said that, and guilt gnawed at my gut almost as much as confusion tangled my thoughts. I wanted to apologize to him for it, but then what? I'd be in his presence with forgiveness on the table. Where the hell did we go from there?

"I'm sorry I threw your dead boyfriend in your face, but I still won't take you back. Have a nice life."

Assuming, of course, he wanted me back, and I didn't know if he did or not, which was unusual for Luke. It wasn't just a different step; it was an altogether different dance. He'd extended the olive branch without asking for anything in return except a tattoo and forgiveness.

I dipped the tattoo needle in the red ink and kept trying to focus on that and nothing else. Fat chance. Luke was on my mind and there he'd stay until this was somehow resolved or he faded into my past again.

I wanted to believe he'd changed, that with time and maturity had come repentance. I wanted to believe that, but he'd "changed" so many times before. That, and he could be so calm and cool when he lied, so smooth and unflinching in his deception. I'd often wondered if he was one of those people who could fool a polygraph.

God only knew he'd fooled me enough times. If not with his alibis, then his explanations. If not explanations, then promises to change.

I rinsed the tattoo needle and dipped it in pale blue ink. As I continued working, I thought back to the waning days of our relationship, when the truth had slapped me in the face enough times that I could no longer deny its existence or how much it hurt.

One particular memory worked its way to the surface. It was a Sunday morning, and I'd sat out on the balcony with the sunrise, a half-smoked pack of Marlboros, and the latest copy of the local apartment guide. As I lit another cigarette —Christ, I'd had far too many already—I glared at the guide. It hadn't had much good news for me that morning. What I could afford was unavailable. What was available, I couldn't afford. There was no way in hell I'd be able to live on my own and still be close to the classes I sometimes attended and the tattoo shop where I apprenticed.

My options were limited. Find a roommate, move back in with my parents on the other side of town, or stay here. I was iffy about the first two options, but the third was rapidly sliding into "no way in hell" territory.

I lifted my cigarette to my lips again. The hairs on the back of my neck stood on end, and I paused mid-drag. A second later, the sliding glass door opened behind me. I casually slid the apartment guide into my jacket and out of sight.

I looked over my shoulder as Luke closed the slider. He offered a weak, sleepy smile and sank into the other chair. As he pulled a wrinkled pack of cigarettes from his pocket and plucked my lighter off the table, I watched him through a stream of exhaled smoke.

"So, how was the party?" I asked.

He shrugged. "Wasn't the greatest I've ever attended, but it was fun," he said around the cigarette resting loosely in the corner of his lips. He lit it, took a drag, then tilted his head back and blew out a stream of smoke.

"Usual crowd?"

He nodded, chuckling. "Same people, same stupid drunk shit."

"Anything exciting happen?"

He didn't even flinch. Didn't hesitate, didn't bat an eye. "No, not that I saw. I spent most of the evening just hanging out and trying to gently let Alex Reiner know I'm not available."

I laughed dryly and crushed my cigarette in the ashtray. "He still hasn't gotten the message?"

He shook his head. "Stubborn fucker." He pulled some more smoke into his lungs. "Flattering and all, but no."

"He'll get the message eventually," I said through gritted teeth. "Well, I'm glad you had a good time."

"Pity you couldn't make it." He smiled and reached across the wobbly plastic table to lace his fingers between mine. "It's never quite the same without you."

I forced a smile, fighting the urge to jerk my hand away. "Maybe next time."

"Did you get any studying done?"

"Not as much as I needed to." Oh, wasn't *that* the truth.

"You still want to go out tonight?"

I chewed the inside of my cheek. "I should probably stay in. Exam on Monday. You know how that goes."

"Yeah, I do."

We smoked in silence for a few minutes. Plenty of questions that doubled as thinly veiled accusations rested on my tongue, but I'd heard enough already. After a while, he extinguished his cigarette and stood.

"I could go for some breakfast," he said. "You?"

I shook my head. "Already ate." Hey, if he could lie without flinching like that, then what was a little white lie from me? I pulled another cigarette out. "I'm going to have another smoke."

"Another one?" He raised an eyebrow. "Jesus, Seb, you're practically chain-smoking these days."

And you're a fucking slut, so kiss my ass. "Only two packs a day."

"You were only smoking one a year ago."

"Bitch at me when I'm up to three," I snapped.

He put his hands up and took a step back. "Okay, okay. I was just concerned."

I glared at him over my cupped hand and lit my cigarette. He narrowed his eyes a little, and I could almost hear him weighing the pros and cons of getting on my case for both my attitude and my smoking.

Go ahead. I took a long drag, not breaking eye contact as I released the smoke out of the corner of my mouth. *I dare you.*

Either he just wasn't in the mood to argue or he sensed more trouble brewing beneath the surface, but he wisely thought better of saying anything more.

Without another word, he went back inside. The sliding glass door closed, and my shoulders dropped. The cigarette between my fingers smoldered, the featherweight tobacco and paper suddenly leaden in my hand. Even if it wasn't as heavy as the weight on my shoulders, I still couldn't bring it to my lips.

I desperately wanted some more nicotine in my already saturated system, but I had my lips pressed together too tightly to accommodate a cigarette. The only thing I wanted more than another lungful of smoke was not to break down in tears, and the latter was becoming increasingly likely.

I couldn't decide what hurt more: the fact that he was cheating on me again, or his ability to casually look me in the eye and lie about it.

Not that I'd been completely honest with him. Maybe two wrongs didn't make a right, but I couldn't help thinking I was justified in my dishonesty.

I wondered if I should tip my hand or let him keep lying until he tripped over his own tangled web. I supposed I could just fess up and tell him I knew full well that Alex Reiner hadn't been fawning all over him at the party and trying to get into his pants.

Alex Reiner wasn't at the party.

Nor was Luke.

Well, they were there for a little while, but they left early.

They left early together.

About forty-five minutes before I arrived.

I shoved the cigarette into the ashtray so hard I nearly knocked the wobbly plastic table over. Then I pulled the apartment guide out from under my jacket and flipped through it for the hundredth time since sunrise.

The tattoo needle hit a particularly sensitive spot near a bone, and the intense sting startled me back into the present. I cursed under my breath, took my foot off the pedal and set the needle down. I sat back, cocking my head to one side, then the other, to work a crick out of my neck.

Staring up at the ceiling, I blew out a breath. I never did call any of the apartments in that guide. I'd confronted him later that day, and in true Luke form, he'd turned on the charm. We'd followed the same old script. He'd apologized, he'd groveled, and eventually I'd forgiven him just as I always had.

Six months later, he left me for someone else, and that was that until he showed up in my shop to get his tattoo.

I looked at my own partially shaded tattoo, and just couldn't work up the enthusiasm to finish it tonight. I bandaged my arm, cleared my workstation and closed everything down for the night. With the shop locked up, the lights turned off and my mind a million miles away, I headed across the street to my apartment.

Just getting up the stairs to the second floor required energy I didn't have. I made it eventually, though, and keyed myself in. Tossed my keys on the kitchen counter as I walked by. Didn't bother stopping to pick them up when they slid off the edge and onto the floor with a metallic crunch. Dropped onto the sofa. Rested my forehead in my hand.

Fuck. How the hell was I supposed to get this out of my mind?

I could call him. Apologize for what I said. Leave the door open for him to say whatever it was he still had to say, if anything. Or just apologize and leave it at that.

Or I could let it go. Let it fade into the past like it had before.

Or I could...*what, Seb? What else is there?*

I need a smoke. Oh my fucking God, I need a smoke.

The unopened pack of Marlboros had been taunting me

from the coffee table since the morning after I'd slept with Luke, and there they were now, in all their unmoving, inanimate glory. Waiting to be thrown away. Or smoked.

"Oh, what the hell?" I muttered. With a defeated sigh, I grabbed the pack and lighter off the table and went out onto the patio.

In my absentmindedness, I damn near tamped the pack against my freshly inked right wrist. The bandage caught my eye, though, and not a moment too soon. I switched the pack to my right hand and slapped it against my left. Off with the cellophane, open with the lid, out with the cigarette.

Just the end between my lips was enough to send a shudder down my spine. *Yes, this is what I need.* With a shaking hand, I flicked the lighter and lit the cigarette.

I closed my eyes and took a long drag. The smoky, ash taste was stronger than I remembered, and my eyes watered as the smoke met the back of my throat.

In seconds, the nicotine hit my system. I tilted my head back and exhaled, savoring the rush. It was only because it was my first cigarette in months that it gave me any kind of high. Any one I smoked after this would simply soothe the craving, appease the need and relax my wound-up nerves.

It didn't settle my nerves, though. A first cigarette after this long should have, but it didn't. The nerves I needed to calm were beyond nicotine's reach.

I tapped the ashes into the ashtray on the railing. A half inch or so of rain had accumulated in it since the last time I'd used it, and the falling ashes hissed and sizzled as they hit the water.

I stared at the half-smoked cigarette between my fingers, watching the end smolder and the smoke rise in a twirling transparent wisp of gray.

There was only one thing that stood a chance of settling these frayed and tangled nerves, and that one thing didn't come wrapped in paper and cellophane.

I snuffed out the cigarette in the waterlogged ashtray and went inside to get my keys.

CHAPTER 10

I PARKED IN FRONT OF LUKE'S BUILDING. THERE WAS A car in the reserved spot marked with his apartment number, so presumably he was home. Alone, I hoped.

With my hands in my pockets and my heart in my throat, I walked up to his front door, trying not to think of the last time I'd made this same walk under very different circumstances.

At the door, I took a deep breath. Bracing myself for whatever came of this, I freed my hand from my pocket and knocked.

A moment later, he opened the door and jumped. "Seb. This is, um, unexpected."

"I know, I'm..." I dropped my gaze. "Can we talk?"

"Yeah, sure." He stepped aside, gesturing for me to come in.

He closed the door, and we stood there, looking anywhere but at each other for a moment. In the same place where a passionate embrace hadn't been close enough once, but now an arm's length was too close. Then he nodded toward the living room. Our footsteps echoed through the otherwise silent hallway.

In the living room, I took a seat on one end of the couch. He eased himself into the recliner. A safe distance apart, still close enough for a—hopefully—civil conversation.

I ran a hand through my hair. "Listen, what I said last night. About A.J." I paused. "I'm sorry, Luke, I didn't mean to go there." I released a long breath. "I lost my head. I'm sorry."

He made a dismissive gesture. "You didn't know."

"I still shouldn't have said it. Obviously he was someone important to you, and..." I shook my head. "I'm sorry, I shouldn't have gone there." I swallowed hard. "I didn't mean to hurt you."

"I know you didn't." He offered a slight smile. "It's never been in your nature to hurt someone."

I sighed. That didn't make me feel a hell of a lot better. "I also jumped the gun at the shop when you tried to apologize. I shouldn't have snapped at you like that."

He nodded. "It's okay. Honestly." He paused. "I meant what I said, Seb. That I came to you in the first place to apologize for everything."

"I believe you, I just..." I chewed my lip. "Look, this is all, it's been overwhelming. You walked back into my life out of nowhere, wanted me to tattoo you, and the next thing I knew, we were in bed. And I...it just felt too much like where we were before."

Another nod. "I know. It's been overwhelming for me too. I didn't expect this. Any of it."

I raised an eyebrow.

Luke pursed his lips. "I know you're not in the habit of believing me," he said quietly, "and I can't blame you for that, but honestly, I didn't expect this to happen."

"What do you mean?"

"For us to..." He hesitated. "For us to end up in bed together, and whatever happened in the shop last night, and...well, this." He gestured back and forth between us. "Whatever the hell is going on."

"What *did* you expect to happen?"

He shook his head. "I don't know. I just didn't think we'd be...here."

I said nothing for a moment. "Why now, Luke? After all this time?"

Luke rested his elbow on his knee and his forehead in his hand. "I've been trying to work up the nerve to get in touch with you for a long time. The last couple of years at least." Sighing, he closed his eyes. The room was silent except for my heartbeat as I watched him. As I waited.

Finally, I whispered, "What changed?"

He didn't speak. He didn't move. I could barely breathe, unsure if I was prepared for the answer that furrowed his brow and hadn't yet left his lips.

All at once, he came to life, pushing himself to his feet. I watched in silence as he walked across the room to a bookshelf. He plucked a framed photo from the shelf and held it in both hands, silently staring at the picture, which I couldn't see. I didn't have to ask who was in it, and my heart pounded. I wasn't sure I was ready to see his face.

But whether I was ready or not, Luke came back to this side of the living room. Still holding the photo, he sank onto the couch beside me. He turned the frame so I could see it, tilting it enough to be rid of the glare from the end table light.

It was a snapshot of himself with a blonde woman. Arms slung around each other's shoulders, champagne glasses in their free hands with a *Happy New Year* banner in the background.

"Her name was Anna," he whispered. "Anna James."

I swallowed. "A.J."

He nodded. "I met her a few months after we broke up. Right after I broke up with Gavin." He paused, face coloring slightly. "Gavin was the—"

"I know." The interjection came out sharper than I'd intended, and we both flinched. Gentler now, I said, "I know who Gavin was. Go on."

He took a breath. "A.J. was an amazing woman, Seb. I could talk to her about anything and everything, and I've never known someone to grab life by the balls the way she did. She was..." He closed his eyes and said nothing for a while. Then he went on, "She would have made someone a very happy man, let me tell you."

"What happened to her?" I asked.

Luke set the frame on the coffee table. He leaned back on the couch and ran a hand through his hair, eyes unfocused. Then he gestured at the picture. "That was last year. Right before she shipped out to Iraq."

I didn't ask him to elaborate. The gory details were unnecessary.

After a moment, Luke continued. "She's the only one I ever spoke to about you. Well, I mean, I talked about you, but not like I did with her. I told her what really happened. I told her I regretted how much I hurt you, and that if I had it to do over..." He swallowed. Took a breath. "Anyway, she spent the last couple of years trying to convince me to get in touch with you and make amends. She said it would probably help you and me both sleep a little better at night. And really, I had nothing to lose, you know?" He laughed softly, and it was a sad, hollow sound. "Life is short, after all."

I chewed the inside of my cheek. "So she was...?" I wasn't sure how to phrase the question. I'd never known Luke to be bisexual, but we were young then. He could have figured it out after we'd split.

As if he could read my mind, he said, "She was a *friend*, Seb. Not some lover I was trying to throw in your face. I might have done something petty and obnoxious like that in the past, but not now." He released a long, ragged breath. "She was my best friend, and after I lost her..."

"So, this was all because..." I searched his eyes, choosing my words carefully so it didn't come across as an accusation. "Because you felt like you owed it to her?"

"No." He held my gaze. "I came to you because she was *right*." He reached for my hand, placing his tentatively over mine and watching my eyes. When I didn't push him away, he let it rest there. "Her philosophy was that there was nothing to lose. The worst you could have done was turned me away. The best, you'd forgive me and we could both move on." He looked at our hands, then lifted his off mine and retracted it slowly. "I don't think even she saw this coming."

"I don't know if anyone could have. Whatever the hell this is."

He nodded but didn't speak for a while. "Honestly, I almost didn't come to you when I wanted to get a memorial tattoo for her. I went to every shop in Seattle, but I just didn't feel right about any of them." He looked at me. "You don't know how many times I stopped by your shop before I finally got up the nerve to go in."

My mouth went dry. "You didn't seem nervous when you came in."

He laughed. "I was. I just didn't let it show. And when I

saw you..." He trailed off, shaking his head. "Jesus, Seb, when I saw you, I couldn't even think."

A pang of guilt hit me in the chest as I remembered all the things I'd thought when he showed up at the shop. Of course I couldn't have known the truth at the time, but just knowing I'd thought that way at all killed me. He'd seemed so cocky, so damned self-assured while I'd flailed and struggled to find my footing. How was I to know then that he felt this way?

The silence probably unnerved him. It always did, and like he often did, he filled it. "Listen, I'm not telling you this to make you feel sorry for me, or try to win you over with some sob story. That's why I didn't tell you any of this before. I didn't want you to think..." He cleared his throat. "Anyway, that's just how it happened. She tried to convince me to get in touch with you, and I'd promised her I would eventually. Once I got up the nerve, and believe me, I've been trying for a long time. So I guess it just seemed...appropriate. You know, to come to you when I wanted to get her tattoo. I just..."

I touched his knee. "What?"

"When I came into the shop, I wanted the tattoo, and I wanted to apologize to you for how I treated you. I wasn't there to try to get you into bed or win you back. I just wanted you to know and hoped you could forgive me, but..." He looked me in the eye. "Seb, I had no idea how much I still loved you."

My tongue stuck to the roof of my mouth. I wanted so badly to believe him. I wanted just as badly *not* to believe it so I could walk out of here and never look back.

He shifted slightly, wringing his hands in his lap. "Seb, say something. Give me something here."

I moistened my lips. "Why did you do it?"

He furrowed his brow. "I just told you. I—"

"No," I whispered. "Not that." With a great deal of effort, I held his gaze. "Back then. When you..." I swallowed.

"When I cheated on you?"

I nodded.

His cheeks darkened a little, and he dropped his gaze. "Because I was stupid." He shook his head. "There's no rational, reasonable excuse, Seb. I was stupid. That's all there is to it." He looked me in the eye again. "I was stupid, and I screwed something up that no one in their right mind would have screwed up."

I chewed the inside of my cheek, unsure just what to say.

Luke went on. "I swear to God, I—" His voice cracked, and he paused. After a moment, he spoke again, barely whispering. "I have never regretted anything more in my life than hurting you." He took a breath. "And I'm sorry. For all of it. More than you can even imagine."

I took a moment to let it all sink in before I finally said, "Why a tattoo?"

"What do you mean?"

I shifted, trying not to wring my hands. "Instead of calling, or just coming in. Once we'd started on the tattoo, you were pretty much stuck with me until it was done, so..."

"I know. I was going to get it anyway, and I honestly couldn't imagine anyone but you doing it, so I figured that would also get us in the same room."

"Captive audience?"

He laughed softly. "Yeah, kind of." He bit his lip. "I figured once we were there, maybe I could work up the nerve to tell you all of this. *Not* to suggest going to Wilde's."

"But, what about the way you looked at me when you came in? The first day?"

He managed a shy laugh, avoiding my eyes. "What can I say, Seb? You looked good." His eyebrows lifted and a cautious smile curled his lips. "You looked really good."

Likewise, Luke. Believe me.

His smile faded, and he dropped his gaze to his wringing hands.

"There's something else," he whispered. "And it'll probably piss you off at first, but please, just hear me out."

I nodded slowly, the knots in my stomach tightening. "Okay. Go ahead."

"I didn't feel guilty about cheating on you back then," he said quietly. "Or all the times I promised not to do it again and talked you into taking me back." He paused, glancing at me.

I clenched my jaw, resisting the urge to lash out at him, but I said I'd hear him out, so I kept my mouth shut. *Tightly* shut.

He cleared his throat. "It was the last time that did my conscience in. Maybe it was some long overdue maturity, maybe it was because it was the longest we'd gone without getting back together after breaking up, but it started eating at me. The longer it went on, the more I missed you, and the more I realized I'd done you horribly wrong from the start." He closed his eyes for a second. His Adam's apple bobbed once and then he went on. "When I realized what I'd lost, I was scared to come back and even try to apologize because I was afraid the one time I really, really meant it—" His voice cracked, and he paused, clearing his throat again before continuing. "I was afraid that would be the one time you'd finally had enough and told me to fuck off for the last time. Which I certainly deserved at that point, I just..." He looked at me. "I didn't think I could face you again because I finally knew just how much I'd hurt you and just how much you had every right to hate me."

I swallowed the lump that tried to rise in my throat. I opened my mouth to tell him that no, I didn't hate him, but he spoke before I could.

"And I can't make you believe this, but the God's honest truth is that it has never been as good with anyone else as it was with you. Not just the sex. Everything. And if I'd had half a brain back then, I'd have held on to you and never thought twice about it." He grimaced as if he thought I'd flip out at him. When I didn't, when I didn't speak at all, he whispered, "I guess that's all there is to say."

I bit my lip. Taking a deep breath, I shook my head. "No, it's not." I reached for his face. His eyes flicked back and forth between my hand and my eyes. We both drew sharp breaths when his cheek warmed my palm, and when I brushed the pad of my thumb across his cheekbone, he turned and kissed my hand. I shivered at the gentle touch of his lips to my skin.

Sliding my hand into his hair, I leaned in closer and drew him to me.

Just before our lips met, I whispered, "I love you."

His lips curved into a smile against mine. "I love you too."

CHAPTER 11

My entire universe was condensed into this space, this kiss. This wasn't what I came for, but no quiet, dissenting voice protested, and I wouldn't have listened if it had.

Luke slid his hand under my jacket and pushed it over my shoulder. As his hand followed my jacket down my arm, I half shrugged, half shivered, deepening the kiss as we got rid of the first layer of clothing. The next to go was his shirt. He took it off and dropped it behind him on the couch, and I had to touch him. Now. Right now.

I put my arm around his waist, surprised my fingertips didn't sizzle when they met the heat of his body, and I silently cursed the bandage that kept skin from skin. Cradling the side of his neck with my free hand, I bent and kissed the other side. I dragged my lower lip across the skin just beneath his ear, and he shivered. I trailed my fingers down his back and yes, there they were, the goose bumps that always followed that touch.

He put his hand over mine on his neck. I splayed my fingers so his could lace between mine, and he sucked in a breath as my fingertips moved across his skin. I inhaled deeply, drawing in the scent of him, and for once I didn't hurt or regret at the taste of his skin and the smell of his cologne. This was right.

Luke brought my hand up and kissed my palm, then the heel of my hand, then that deliciously sensitive spot on the inside of my wrist. He drew a gentle circle there with the tip of his tongue, and I did the same just beneath his jaw. We both shivered this time, which only served to bring our bodies closer together.

I raised my head. Our eyes met.

No guilt. No regret. This was right where we needed to be.

When our lips met this time, his kiss had never been so gentle. The tenderness of his mouth and his hands nearly brought tears to my closed eyes. If I hadn't believed his apology was sincere, I did now, because there was more truth in this long, sensual kiss than there had ever been between us. Time had changed us. Him, me, us. The only thing it hadn't done was diminish the way I felt for him or the way I wanted him.

"Let's go in the bedroom," he whispered.

Anticipation sent chills through me. I nodded and we separated.

We rose. Both on our feet now, with our destination known, we stopped and looked at each other. I searched his eyes for second thoughts. He probably searched mine for the same, and if he could have read my mind, he'd have found some. I had doubts. I had many, but my desire for him was stronger.

If he saw those doubts, he said nothing. He took my hand, and my heartbeat drowned out my footsteps on the way down the hall.

Still partly dressed, we sank into bed together, tangled up in arms and long, deep kisses. There was too much fabric, though, too many thick barriers between his skin and mine, and they needed to go.

Undressing this close together was never a graceful procedure, and we tripped over each other every step of the way. As I kicked off my shoe, I caught his shin with my heel. We couldn't get our hands out of each other's way as we unbuckled belts and unzipped jeans. Somewhere amidst getting out of our respective jeans, his kneecap cracked against mine.

"Damn it, sorry," he murmured, his lip brushing mine.

"Don't worry about it." I tried not to make my wince too obvious.

We still kissed whenever our clumsy maneuvers would allow it. Still touched whenever a hand wasn't needed for a belt or a stubborn shoelace. With the clothes finally out of the way, there was more kissing and less fumbling. That is until he slid his hand down my side, over my hip and onto my cock.

We tried to kiss. Missed. Tried again with a little more success.

"This is crazy," he whispered, laughing softly against my lips, "I want you so damned bad, I feel like I don't even know what I'm doing."

"That makes two of us. But you're—" I sucked in a breath as he squeezed gently. "Fuck, Luke, you're doing *just* fine."

He grinned and kissed me, this time taking possession of my mouth with no hesitation, no clumsiness. I cupped his face in both hands and returned his kiss, faltering each time his hand sent another set of icy-hot lightning bolts up my spine.

All at once, he broke the kiss.

"I don't want to wait." He released me and leaned away, returning a second later with a condom in hand. As he cursed and struggled with the condom wrapper, I couldn't help smiling to myself. It was our first time all over again in all its nervous, clumsy perfection.

The condom wrapper finally gave, splitting open at his command. While he put on the condom, I reached for the lube. I poured some into my hand, then nudged his hand out of the way.

"What are— Oh, God." He groaned and closed his eyes as I stroked the lube on, squeezing here, releasing there, just the way I knew he liked it. He let his head fall forward, uneven breaths slipping through parted lips. Finally, he grabbed my wrist. I didn't even flinch when he pressed into my tender tattoo, especially when he whispered, "I can't wait."

I opened my hand, grinning when he gasped at the sudden lack of contact. "I'm not stopping you," I said.

"Good." He sat up and guided his cock to me. I don't know if he screwed his eyes shut while he pushed into me slowly, or if he watched with wide-eyed wonderment as he often did. As much as I loved to watch his face when he took that first stroke, the sensation was just too intense this time. We were really here, we were really doing this. We'd really come back to each other, and I couldn't remember ever being this overwhelmed—physically, emotionally— simply by having him inside me.

"Look at me, Seb," he whispered.

I opened my eyes, blinking them into focus.

He gazed down at me, brow furrowed and eyes locked on mine as he took long, smooth strokes. Even as he picked up speed, as the intensity threatened to force my eyes closed again, I didn't break eye contact. Those beautiful, intense blue eyes, my God, it had been so long since he'd looked at me that way. Since he'd touched me this way, since I'd felt him this way. I didn't want to break eye contact, but if I didn't taste his kiss again...

I slid my hand around the back of his neck and pulled him down to me.

He whimpered into my kiss, and a shudder drove him deeper inside me. With a gasp, he broke the kiss, but he didn't pull away. He moved faster, and our lips still brushed, though it wasn't quite a kiss anymore. Some of our earlier clumsiness came back. We held on to each other, trying to strike the balance between restricting his movement and making enough contact to satisfy our need to touch each other. Eventually we found that balance. Or maybe it just didn't matter; every rhythm he found, every cadence between slow strokes and deep thrusts, was perfect. This was perfect.

His breath caught. When he threw his head back, I went right for his neck, and along with the way he moved inside me, the vibration of his voice and the brush of his stubble and the heat of his skin all conspired against my lips to drive me out of my damned mind. I moaned, burying my face against his neck, and surrendered to the powerful orgasm that wouldn't be denied.

"Oh God, Seb, oh God..." His voice drifted through my delirium, sounding miles away, and his rhythm faltered as he trembled and shuddered. With a deep groan that emerged from the back of his throat, he took one last thrust and released a long, ragged breath as his cock twitched inside me.

When it had all subsided except the aftershocks, I let go of his shoulders. Hell if I could remember when I'd grabbed onto them, or when I'd dug my fingers in quite so hard, but I had, and he didn't seem to mind. We separated slowly, both shivering as he pulled out.

Once the condom and tissues were discarded, we collapsed onto the bed to catch our breath. He raised himself up on one elbow and touched my face with his other hand.

"I love you," he whispered.

"I love you too." I did, and I believed him, but I was scared. Combing my fingers through his hair, I looked up at him, and for the first time, that dissenting voice crept into the back of my mind. *What if...?*

He moistened his lips and tilted his head slightly. "What's wrong?"

I shifted my gaze away from him. "Just...worried, I guess."

He trailed the backs of his fingers across my cheek. "What about?" Then enlightenment seemed to strike, and he sighed. "You're worried about doing this again?"

I nodded. "I know it's been a long time, and we've both changed, but I..." I looked at him. "You have to understand where I'm coming from when I question whether or not I'm setting myself up to go through hell again."

He flinched but nodded. "I know. And I do understand. I wish I'd never given you a reason to doubt me like that, but I'm not holding it against you."

"So where do we go from here?"

He shook his head. "I don't know. It's up to you. I think you know what I want, but..." He raised his eyebrows.

I took a breath. "I can't promise anything overnight, Luke." I ran my fingers through his hair. "It's not that I'm trying to hold a grudge or hang on to the past, but..." I bit my lip. "The fact is, we do have a history."

"I know." He trailed his fingertips down the side of my neck. "I don't expect you to pretend nothing ever happened before." He leaned forward and kissed me lightly. "We'll just take it a day at a time. Give me today. If you still feel the same way about me in the morning, then give me tomorrow. And..." He paused, shrugging with one shoulder. "We'll just see where it goes."

"I think I can do that." I smiled, letting my fingertips drift over the back of his neck until he shivered. "And I think I like where we're starting today."

He grinned. "In bed?"

"Damn right." I pulled him to me.

I gave him today.

I'd give him tonight.

And I hoped, from the bottom of my heart, that I'd give him tomorrow.

EPILOGUE

BIRMINGHAM, ALABAMA

About a year later

Neither of us spoke on the way down the winding concrete path. In one hand, Luke carried a long stem yellow rose. The other loosely grasped my hand.

Up ahead, the path split. He didn't hesitate.

"This way," he whispered, gesturing to the left. We followed the meandering concrete a few more yards before he nodded toward an area of the carefully manicured lawn on the right. We left the path and walked across the grass past flowers, miniature American flags and names.

Toward the end of a row, his gait slowed.

I ran my thumb along the back of his. *I'm here.*

He squeezed my hand. *I know.*

We stopped, and Luke gently freed his hand from mine. He knelt and laid the flower beside the headstone. Then he ran his fingers across the granite lettering.

SSgt. Anna Marie James, USMC
January 11, 1979—April 17, 2010
Daughter. Sister. Soldier. Friend.

Beside the inscription was an angel similar to the one I'd tattooed on Luke's arm. Carved in stone, carved in flesh, as if her loved ones were afraid she'd fade away, that she'd be forgotten.

There was no chance of that. I'd seen her only in photos, but she'd tattooed herself across my life in ways she'd probably never imagined. It was because of her that I'd found my footing again, that I was—after some much-needed time and maturity on his part and mine—back with the man I loved. A.J. was a stranger to me, but I'd never forget her. Nor, I was sure, would anyone who'd ever known her.

Luke had told me about her. Late at night, while we sat on my back balcony on mismatched plastic patio furniture, burning citronella candles instead of cigarettes while we drank a beer or two in her memory. He'd told me about her love of pranks, practical jokes and trying everything once. About the time she convinced him to go skydiving with her in spite of his fears and reservations, and how they'd never quite gotten around to doing it again. About how she'd put up with his moods while he was quitting smoking and threatened him with bodily harm if he ever lit up again.

Talking about her made it easier for him to deal with her being gone, and it gave us something to talk about when the topic of "us" was just too incendiary.

The last year hadn't been all sunshine, roses and nights

on the balcony. We'd taken it a day at a time, as Luke had suggested, and there were quite a few times when I questioned whether our relationship had any tomorrows left. Trust is a tricky thing to build, an even trickier one to *re*build, and we'd had our fair share of heated fights and long, uncomfortable discussions while we worked out the bugs.

Over the last few months, though, the dust had more or less settled. Now we spent less time arguing and more time in each other's arms. Enjoying each other's company. Being together like we'd never had a reason to be apart. There was some discussion of moving in together, but we weren't rushing it. We'd get there.

I squeezed his shoulder gently and he put his hand over mine. This was the first time he'd been to her gravesite since the funeral. The first time I'd been here at all. I doubted it would be the last time for either of us.

Luke sighed as he rose slowly. He cleared his throat once, then again, and blinked a few times, but not before I saw the hint of tears.

I put my arm around his waist. "You okay?"

He looked at the headstone for a moment, then turned to me and managed a smile. "Yeah, I'm okay."

"Do you want to stay a while?"

"No, I..." His gaze flicked back down to the headstone. Our eyes met again. "No, I think I'm good."

"You sure?"

"Yeah." He nodded toward the cement path that had brought us here. "You ready to go?"

"Whenever you are."

Hand in hand, we started back toward the path and followed it the way we'd come. We both stopped and glanced over our shoulders one last time before A.J.'s resting place was out of sight. Then we looked at each other. Luke touched my face and tenderly kissed my forehead. After a moment, we kept walking.

Don't worry, A.J. You won't be forgotten.

THE WILDE'S SERIES CONTINUES!

THE CLOSER YOU GET

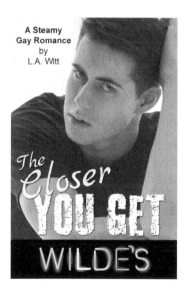

A Steamy
Gay Romance
by
L.A. Witt

The *Closer*
YOU GET

WILDE'S

THE CLOSER YOU GET

The virgin isn't the only one with something to lose...

Self-described manwhore Kieran Frost is loving the single life. Two years after moving to Seattle, he still has his friends with benefits, Rhett and Ethan, plus a never-ending supply of gorgeous, available men wandering through the bar where he works. A relationship? Spare him the drama and heartbreak. He's got no complaints about his unattached lifestyle.

When Rhett's daughter introduces him to newly-out-of-the-closet Alex Corbin, Kieran's interest perks up. After all, the quiet ones are always the freaks in bed. But Alex isn't just shy and reserved. He's a virgin in every sense of the word—he's never even kissed anyone.

Kieran is no one's teacher, and his first instinct is to run like hell in the other direction. But his conscience won't let him throw the naïve kid to the wolves for someone else to take advantage of. The plan is to introduce Alex to his own sexuality, pull him out of his shell, then go their separate ways.

It's the perfect, foolproof plan...assuming no one falls in love.

This 68,000 word novel was previously published.

Available on Amazon.

MEET ME IN THE MIDDLE

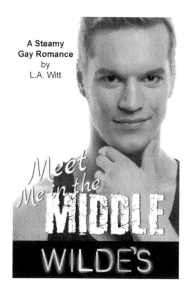

A Steamy
Gay Romance
by
L.A. Witt

MEET ME IN THE MIDDLE

Fool me three times...

Dale Ramsey is looking forward to his twenty-year high school reunion except for one small problem: will his old friend – and old flame – be there?

Adam O'Connor has disappeared twice from Dale's life. Once after a graduation night fling, and again after a hot reunion years later. When he resurfaces this time, single and on the verge of retiring from the Navy, he wants to mend fences with Dale. Mend fences and maybe tear up some sheets.

The spark between them is alive and well, but Dale resists. After all, Adam has only been interested in him before when his life has been in flux, just like it is now, and Dale refuses to be anyone's placeholder until something better comes along. He wants his friend back, but he's not looking to be deserted a third time.

Over and over, though, their attempts to rekindle their friendship wind up igniting something much hotter, and Dale's feelings for Adam are far too strong to ignore. Should he put himself on the line and risk another broken heart? Or should he be the one to walk away this time?

This 55,000 word novel was previously published.

Available on Amazon.

ABOUT THE AUTHOR

L.A. Witt and her husband have been exiled from Spain and sent to live in Maine because rhymes are fun. She now divides her time between writing, assuring people she is aware that Maine is cold, wondering where to put her next tattoo, and trying to reason with a surly Maine coon. Rumor has it her arch nemesis, Lauren Gallagher, is also somewhere in the wilds of New England, which is why L.A. is also spending a portion of her time training a team of spec ops lobsters. Authors Ann Gallagher and Lori A. Witt have been asked to assist in lobster training, but they "have books to write" and "need to focus on our careers" and "don't you think this rivalry has gotten a little out of hand?" They're probably just helping Lauren raise her army of squirrels trained to ride moose into battle.

Website: www.gallagherwitt.com
Email: gallagherwitt@gmail.com
Twitter: @GallagherWitt